Poverty Flat

Poverty Flat

By Major Mitchell

Shalako Press Oakdale, CA

Poverty Flat

All rights reserved

© Copyright 2007 by Major Mitchell

This is a work of fiction.
All characters and events portrayed in this book are fictional,
and any resemblance to real people is purely
coincidental.

Reproduction in any manner, in whole or part,
in English or in any other languages, or otherwise
without the written permission of the publisher
is prohibited.

For information contact:
Shalako Press
P.O. Box 371
Oakdale, CA 95361-0371
www.majormitchell.net

ISBN:

Cover photograph: Debbi Mitchell
Cover design: Karen Borrelli
Editor: Judith Mitchell

PRINTED IN THE UNITED STATES OF AMERICA

Acknowledgments

This book is a combined effort of many people. I would first like to thank Patricia Snoke and the Gustine Historical Society for helping in the research of Poverty Flat, Hills Ferry and the many places mentioned in this book.

I would also like to thank Kelly Phillips, Jamie Hook, Vanessa Jackson, Janet Bly, and the several other people who read the manuscript, caught the author's mistakes, and offered their input.

A big thanks to our daughter, Debbi Mitchell, for the cover photograph.

Most of all, hugs and kisses to my wife and partner, Judy, who's editing always turns my hieroglyphics into something readable.

*To Judy,
for indulging my writing habit through the years*

Poverty Flat

What Christian Baker had been looking for was a dry place to spend the night and weather out the storm. What he got was a frightened woman and a little boy holed inside a leaky cabin. That wouldn't have been a bad thing in itself, except the woman had a shotgun, and kept waving it in his face and yelling things that Chris had trouble understanding.

It had been raining steady for four days when he discovered the cabin. His shoulder-length brown hair lay plastered against his oilcloth slicker, while water dripped from his moustache and the two-week-old stubble on his chin. His trail-worn clothes were soaked, and water sloshed inside his boots as he dismounted. He grunted as he sank past his ankles in mud, then inhaled a deep breath as he surveyed the countryside from the top of the hill. He believed he was somewhere in the San Joaquin Valley, but had no clue where that was in conjunction to anything. The truth was, Captain Christian Baker was lost, but even that didn't matter at the moment. The only question in his mind was if the tiny farmhouse was safe. He wanted to get out of the rain, build a fire, and dry out. California hadn't impressed him, and he was wondering what all the fuss was about.

"Doesn't look like much, does it?" he said. The horse answered with a snort and gave him a shove with his nose, before starting toward the ramshackle barn.

"Yeah, guess you're right. Even if the roof leaks and there's a grizzly bear inside, it's bound to be better than wading in mud. Any old bear's just gonna have to move over and give us some room."

It was getting dark and he paused near a window to listen. Not seeing or hearing anything, he decided the place must be abandoned, and was surprised to find a couple of chickens and a poor excuse for a milk cow inside the barn. After turning his mustang, Bruiser, loose in an empty stall and removing his saddle, he took a look around. He couldn't really call it a barn, when he had shucked down to the cob, as his father used to say. It was more of a lean-to with boards covering three sides, and no doors to block the wind whipping around the corner. The roof leaked a steady stream that caused the cow to keep toward one side of her stall. Chris scrounged a couple of fistfuls of straw from the floor and gave one to Bruiser and the other to the cow before heading back outside.

"Yeah, I know," he said as the horse snorted his displeasure at Chris's generosity. "But I can eat her if there ain't nothing else, and you can always find a little something outside when it stops raining. Of course, I could eat you, if that's what you want." The horse snorted and shook his head.

"That's what I thought. You'd be too tough anyway, so quit your complaining."

He ducked his lean six-foot four-inch frame under the low porch cover and stamped his muddy boots before pounding on the door. The door crept open on its own accord, so Chris leaned his head near the crack with a hand on the butt of his gun and yelled.

"Anyone home? It's getting kinda wet out here." He waited a long minute and received no answer. He rapped on the door with the gun and yelled once more.

"Okay, I'm coming in. If there's a grizzly bear or skunk inside, you're just gonna have to make room for one wet cowpuncher."

The only sound was the pounding rain and the creaking of the door as he pushed it open. It felt almost as

Poverty Flat

cold inside the cabin as it did in the rain, and he thought it was darker than Dead Horse Cave back home in Georgia. There was an oil lamp on the table, so holstering the gun, he felt inside the slicker for a pack of matches he kept rolled in oilskin. It took a couple of minutes before finding one dry enough to light. He had just struck it, and was starting to light the lamp, when her voice caused him to jump.

"Don't move. I've got you covered with my husband's gun. Put your hands up over your head."

If Chris had learned anything by spending close to six years with Yankee lead flying around his head it was, don't argue when someone's got a gun pointed at you. So, he did exactly like she said.

"Now, turn around...real slow."

"Yes ma'am." He turned to face her. "Ma'am? This here match is getting mighty short. May I light the lamp? Or, do you just want me to drop it?"

"You may light the lamp. But be careful," she added as he removed the globe.

"You don't have to worry, ma'am," he said, adjusting the wick. "That ten-gauge you're holding is something I don't care to argue with." It was hard to see her against the back wall, but he could tell she was young, maybe in her mid-twenties, and scared. Almost as frightened as the boy crowding up against her. Chris guessed him to be about seven, maybe eight years old, from the look of him. He'd always believed a frightened person was twice as dangerous as someone in their right mind, so he decided his only option was to do exactly what she said.

"What are you doing here? What is it you want?" The barrels swayed in a small circle as she talked.

"Ma'am, please be careful with that thing." He held his hands out, knowing there was no way they could stop a load of double-ought shot. His insides knotted as he watched the end of the barrel move in tiny circles.

"Get your hands up!"

"Yes, ma'am."

3

She moaned and grabbed her stomach with her left hand, lowering the gun a bit.

"You okay, ma'am?" He started around the table but the gun barrel jumped back up.

"Stay where you are, and answer my question. What are you doing here and what do you want?"

"Well, for starters, I'm trying to get out of the rain. And as to what I want, I'm cold and hungry, and in no mood to argue. So, if you don't mind, I'll mosey toward the barn, and sleep with my horse and that old cow." He started toward the door, but stopped as she cried out and doubled over.

"Ma'am, if you're sick, or if something's wrong..." He again started for her, but the shotgun seemed to know exactly where he was.

"Hold it! I want your gun."

"Ma'am?"

"I don't trust you. I want you to take your gun off and leave it here before you go to the barn."

"Yes, ma'am." He unbuckled the gunbelt. "But I got me a saddle gun out in the barn. What about it? Want me to go bring it inside also?" Chris knew it was a stupid thing to say the moment the words left his lips. She began stuttering as her eyes darted around the room like they were searching for something that wasn't there.

"I'm sorry, ma'am, I shouldn't of even mentioned that old gun. Fact is, both my guns are so wet, they probably wouldn't shoot if I wanted them to. I'll tell you what," he held his right hand like he was taking an oath, "I'll just leave this hog-leg here and go fetch that Winchester for you. How'll that be? You can have 'em both right here, while I bed down in the barn. Then, I'll be gone first thing in the morning."

He slid the buckle loose and held it in the lamplight for her to see. He'd just finished wrapping the cartridge belt around the holster when she doubled over and cried "Oh God!" grabbing her stomach with both hands.

Poverty Flat

"Now, you look-a-here, lady. Either you're sick, or something's wrong." He pushed past the table as the boy started tugging on her sleeve. She raised the gun again, but slower this time.

"Don't make me shoot you! I will, so help me God. I will if I have to. Put your hands up."

"Yes, ma'am, you don't have to shoot me." Chris held his gun and holster in his left hand away from his body and raised his right one toward the cobweb-covered ceiling.

"Look here," he continued. "I'll leave it right here on the table for you to get after I'm gone out the door."

"No, don't move. I don't trust you. William," she said to the boy, "get the man's gun."

"No, don't you do it, boy." Chris frowned and shook his head.

"I'll shoot you if I have to."

"Yes, ma'am, I know you will."

"Go get the gun, William."

"Okay, boy, if your mama insists." He held the gun out for him. "But if you don't mind me saying so, lady, that's the stupidest thing I've seen you do yet."

"And how is that, mister whatever your name is? I've got this gun pointed at you and I know how to use it." She took a step closer as he handed the gun to the boy.

"Because, if I had meant you harm, I could have simply grabbed your boy and held my gun on him, or this here knife." He pulled the Arkansas toothpick from its sheath and tossed it on the table. "What would you have done then, lady?"

The question seemed to shake her as she paled and lowered the gun. She backed toward the wall, where she again moaned and bent over. Chris took a step forward but the gun came back up, causing him to freeze where he was.

"You're hurting something fierce, ma'am."

"No, yes...but I'm well enough to use this gun," she said through gritted teeth. She seemed real slow recovering this time.

5

Chris had never claimed to be the smartest man around. The fact was, his brothers, James and Henry, used to say he was slower'n wet gunpowder catching onto things, and he allowed that when it came to women, that might be true. Chris had always been shy around females, and outside of his mother and sisters, had little experience dealing with members of the opposite sex. The truth was, he'd had only one sweetheart up to that point, and it had been several years since last seeing her. But standing there, soaked to the skin, brain-numbed by the cold and shivering, it had taken him longer than usual to decide what was happening. Besides, he reasoned, facing a crazy woman with a shotgun doesn't set a man to thinking right.

"Good, God," he yelled and started toward her. She whipped the shotgun upward and Chris didn't hesitate to snatch it from her grip.

"There's no doubt you know how to use this thing, ma'am. But in a short while, you're going to be in no condition to shoot anyone. Besides, if you kill me, who's going to help you bring that young-un into the world? Where's your husband, anyway?"

"He went into town for supplies, and will be back any minute, so, you had better leave before he gets here." She stared at him with huge dark eyes as she carefully sat herself on the edge of the bed.

"Blamed stupid thing to do," he said, studying the cabin real good for the first time. It wasn't much better than the lean-to that Bruiser and the cow were sleeping in, and not a whole lot bigger. He guessed the cabin to be perhaps ten foot by ten, and as bare as their Georgia farm after the Yankee carpetbaggers had gotten through. There wasn't anything except the home-made bed she was sitting on, an old cot stuck in the opposite corner, the table and one chair. He guessed that one of them had to stand or take turns sitting on the chair or the wooden box he had accidently kicked as he rounded the table searching for something that might help the situation. "Running off in the middle of a storm and leaving a pregnant woman and little boy to fend for themselves…feller like that needs horsewhipping."

"What was that you said about my husband?"

"You heard me." He turned to glare. "I said he needs horsewhipping, leaving you out here like this."

"Well, for your information, neither of us thought I'd be having labor this early. And as you can tell, this house is in dire need of supplies."

"I reckon. Ain't nothing to eat but dust and cobwebs. How long since you and the boy's ett?"

"I don't know if that's any of your concern."

"I'm a-making it my concern. Now answer my question, girl. How long since you and this boy's had anything to eat?"

"We had plenty to eat for supper."

"When? That fireplace ain't been lit all day long. This place is cold enough to store meat for the winter. You didn't eat no supper, so quit lying to me. When was the last time you ett?"

"Supper…yesterday. If it's any of your business."

"Good God in heaven," he said tossing his arms in the air. "Guess it's up to me, then. Ya got any firewood cut and stored anywheres on this place? Or, did he leave you without any of that, too?"

"My husband cut plenty, just before he left." She paused to take a couple of deep breaths as another pain took her. "It's stacked at the rear of the house. I didn't have time to carry any inside before the rain started."

"No, don't reckon you did, seeing as it's been raining for days now. Don't know why he didn't stack it on the porch, like any sensible man would've done. Guess I'd better go fetch some inside," he said, shoving his hat down on his head.

"I didn't ask for your help, mister. You, you can just leave." She yelled and pointed toward the door.

"Yes'm, I reckon I could. But in case you haven't noticed, you're about to have a baby right soon. And I don't reckon I'd like having it on my conscience, knowing I ran off leaving you here like this."

"I can manage by myself, thank you very much."

"Yes, I suppose you could," Chris said, forcing her back onto the bed. "Cows, horses, dogs and polecats all know how to bring their young-uns into the world. And most of 'em, especially the polecats, do it by themselves most of the time. You saying you ain't no better than one of them critters?"

"No, but..."

"Quit arguing with me then." He turned to stare at the boy, who's frozen stance reminded him of the wooden Indian in front of Clem Parker's Tobacco Store back home. "You got any clean water 'round here, boy? I reckon we'd better wash ourselves some."

"Yes, sir." He ran to fetch a wooden bucket from the corner that had about an inch of water in the bottom.

"Well, guess that's a start. Ain't got any more water inside besides this here?" He shook his head and stared wide-eyed.

"We used all there was earlier," the woman said as another pain gripped her. "There's another bucket on the porch, but it's empty."

"You're fixin' to have that young-un real soon, ain't you, ma'am?"

"I'm afraid so." She was breathing hard, so Chris ran to the rear of the house, splashing and slipping through puddles. When he had finished carrying several arm-loads of wood inside, he rolled up his sleeves and scrubbed his grimy paws the best he could. Then, grabbing both buckets, he placed them where a good stream of water was poring off one corner of the roof and told the boy to tote them back inside once they were filled. He hadn't realized he had been grumbling out loud as he stoked a fire, until she asked him what he was saying.

"Nothing, ma'am. Just talking to myself," he said as the flames caught.

"I distinctly heard you say something about me being worse than a wounded mountain lion." She actually grinned before another pain took her. She was a tough little gal, he had to give her that. She scrunched her eyes and gritted her teeth, holding this one inside.

"Well, you gotta admit, facing a scatter-gun wasn't the most pleasant welcome a man might've gotten," he said, pulling the box close to the bed. He studied her a long minute. "My pappy shot an old cougar back in the hills once, but didn't quite kill it. That cat crawled inside a cave amongst the rocks to lick her wounds. One of our hounds ran head-long into that hole after her and got hisself all tore up. We wound up having to kill the dog and cat both before it was over."

"Well, I hope I'm not quite as bad as that. It's just that...I don't even know your name. How do I know you're not...?" She caught her breath and scrunched her face.

"Christian, ma'am. My name is Christian Michael Baker. That's the handle my mama pinned on me. Most folks just call me Chris. Them that like me, that is. Those that don't call me just about everything else. And you did right, ma'am. Being cautious that is."

"Oh, dear Jesus... I'm afraid it's coming." She squeezed her eyes shut and cried out. Chris glanced toward the boy who remained frozen to the floor.

"Better check them buckets, boy. We're gonna need them here right quick. It's about time for you to meet your little brother."

Chapter 2

    All creatures come into this world their own way. Some, like Chris's horse, Bruiser, seem to pop out and quietly look things over, as if everything belongs to them and was just waiting for them to show up. Others cry like they're frightened of being separated from their mothers. Then, there's those that arrive like the one Chris held in his arms. Red in the face, kicking, screaming and flaying both arms as if it was telling everyone to get out of the way. He had guessed wrong about one thing, though. The boy wasn't going to meet any baby brother.
    "Come here, son, and meet your sister," he said, wrapping the little bundle in a blanket.
    "Why's she crying?" He stood wide-eyed staring over Chris' shoulder from where he sat on the box.
    "She's just angry at being disturbed, I reckon."
    "Aren't you going to let me see my own daughter?" The woman half-laughed and half-cried as he placed the squalling bundle in her outstretched arms.
    "Oh, my Lord, she's beautiful," she said.
    "Yes, ma'am. And a real fighter, just like her mother. I shore wish I had some way of painting a picture of y'all just the way you are. A mother holding her new-born daughter. There ain't a more beautiful sight in the whole world."
    "A fighter, Mr. Baker?" she said. Her eyes were dark pools as she stared up at him. "Is that what you think of me?"

"Well, yes'm, I reckon I do. And that scatter-gun will testify that what I'm saying is true."

"I guess I should apologize, except we were frightened by you showing up like you did." She nuzzled her baby as she talked. "I hope you'll forgive me for acting the way I did."

"Ain't nothing to forgive. A woman shouldn't have to apologize for trying to protect her family."

"Thank you. But how does being a fighter make either of us more beautiful? I want her to grow up to be a lady."

"Yes'm," he said, washing his hands in the small pan he'd found hanging on a rusty nail. "But I don't know why she can't be both. Wasn't no woman created that was more of a lady than my mama. But she'd fight 'til her last breath if she thought someone was gonna hurt one of her young-uns. I seen her do it too many times to believe otherwise. I recall the time she took a butter churn to ol' Silas Hawkins, and sent him howling down the road."

"And what, pray tell, did he do to deserve being hit with a butter churn?" she said with a laugh, followed by a yawn. Chris stood there a second staring at the two lying in bed before answering.

"He accused my youngest brother of stealing some melons out of his garden."

"Well, did he do it?"

"Certainly. We all did. Thing was, Silas took it upon himself to whup James with a hickory switch before bringing him home and telling our mama. Of course, James started howling like he was half-dead when he seen Mama, making her think that old man had nearly beat the life out of him. Well, you didn't touch one of that woman's pups, I'll tell you that. She was on the front porch churning butter when they come up. She jerked the handle out of that churn and went to work on that old man. Half-churned butter was flying everywhere as she chased him down the road."

"Oh, my word." She held a hand to her stomach laughing. "Then what happened? Did your brother get away with the ruse?"

"No ma'am. You don't know our mama. She took a wooden spoon to James' backside the instant she got over being mad at old man Hawkins. She never cottoned to any thievery at all, not even innocent melon stealing like all us youn'ns had done one time or the other. Anyway, I reckon that fighting spirit made her all the more beautiful to us Bakers, because we knew, no matter what, we could always run home to mama, and she'd make things right."

"Where is your mother at now, Mr. Baker?" She yawned again.

"Heaven, ma'am. She passed away sometime during the war. I'm just sorry I wasn't there to make the passing easier for her, like she always made things for me."

"I'm so sorry to hear that, Mr. Baker."

"I believe you mean that, ma'am. Now, you'd better feed that young-un her breakfast like a good mama," he said, putting a hand on her son's shoulder. "And try to get some rest. Me and this boy here are going to try and rustle up some grub." He turned toward the door and paused to look back over his shoulder.

"One other thing, ma'am. Seeing as we're sort of acquainted now, would you mind telling me your name?"

"Not at all, Mr. Baker. My name is Mary Ellen Shafer. And I believe you already know that my son is named William."

"Yes, ma'am. He's a fine boy and listens real good. Mind me asking what you're gonna call that new young-un?"

"Edith...Edith Patricia, after my mother."

"Right pretty name, for a right pretty girl. Now you get some rest like I said, while me and William here rustle us up some grub."

"Certainly. William will show you where everything is. And thank you Mr. Baker, for all that you have done."

Chris followed the boy to the barn, hoping they might find a couple of eggs the scrawny chickens might have laid. The heavy rain had stopped, and had turned into a heavy mist now, but the air was turning colder by the minute.

"After we find some grub, we'd better haul all the firewood we can 'round to the front porch. Reckon we're gonna be needing it before this day's over with," he said, buttoning his jacket.

"Look, Mr. Baker. I found one," the boy said holding a brown egg high in the air.

"Be careful with that thing, boy. It's more valuable than gold."

"This egg?" He started laughing as he set it on Bruiser's saddle blanket.

"Yes, sir, that egg." Chris paused from rinsing out the milking bucket to nod. "I seen the time back during the war when a man would've given his shirt right off his back for that egg. Fact is, a man can own a lot of things, but the number one thing he needs, outside his religion, is food." Chris drew up the three-legged stool and began pulling on the cow's udders.

"Well, now ain't that a surprise." He grinned at the boy and continued talking as he pulled on the udders. "I wouldn't of thought she had any milk to give. It ain't much, mind you, but enough for what we need right now."

"I never thought about eggs and things like that before." The boy stared at the egg lying on the blanket as he talked. "I always thought if you were rich, you could eat anything you wanted. That's what my daddy says."

"I guess that might be true in most cases. How old are you, boy?"

"Nine."

"Well, I guess you're old enough to learn one of the great truths of life, then. Money is mighty important to most folks. And, there ain't nothing really wrong with it by itself. But I heard tell of an old trapper back in the hills that folks found holed-up inside his winter cabin with a whole passel of furs and what not. He had enough beaver and fox hides to make him a rich man all by themselves. But when they were going through his things, they found sack after sack of gold. They figured he must've found it somewhere in the creek where he'd been trapping. I reckon that's what caused him to stay holed-up there like he was. Anyway, when the snow set in, he ran out of supplies. That's when he discovered that all the game in those mountains were smarter than he was, and had lit out for warmer ground. All them furs and all that gold didn't do him a lick of good."

"Was he dead?" The boy's eyes grew almost as big as his mother's.

"I hope to shout. Starved clean to death. He wasn't nothing but a dry bag of bones. Now, I'll ask you, what good did all that gold do him?"

"It might have, if he could have gotten to a store."

"The point is, he couldn't," Chris said, patting the cow on the rump. "And the time always comes in a man's life that things don't go like he wants them to. Like your ma in there," he pointed toward the house. "I'll just bet she'd rather have had your daddy around to help with the baby. Or better yet, been in town with a doctor looking out for her. Now, ain't that right?"

"Yes, sir."

"Yet, it didn't turn out that way. And, knowing the type of woman she is, I'll just bet she would have rather fed you some vittles yesterday, instead of seeing you go hungry. In fact, I'll bet she got mighty hungry herself. Ain't that right?"

He nodded.

"First thing a man's got to remember when he starts out in life, is make sure he's sitting right with his maker. Because he never knows when he's going to meet up with him. Second thing is," Chris held up two fingers, "make sure he's packed away enough grub to last him awhile. Because he'll never know where or when he'll be able to buy his next meal. And, lastly," he held three fingers in front of the boy's face, "make sure he's got some sort of roof over his head. Because you can get mighty cold and wet if you're not careful. A man can live and take care of his family if he's got those things. But he can have all the money in the world and still die, if he ain't got them." Chris gave him a long minute to mull the words over before grabbing the milk pail and patting him on the back.

"Better see if you can't find more'n one egg, son. I'll take this here milk and what grub I got stuffed inside my saddlebags back to the house and see if we can't whip some sort of breakfast together for you and your mama."

******

William was able to find two more eggs in the corner of an empty stall, and Chris had some jerked beef, coffee, and cold biscuits stuck inside the bags. He felt a smidgen of shame after lecturing the boy about being prepared, then not having anymore food. But he'd always made it a habit of shooting fresh game to eat along the trail. So, he'd shucked Los Angeles with no more than a few days supplies to last until he got to the next town. Only thing troubling was, he had no idea where the next town was. In fact, he didn't have the slightest clue where this cabin was in conjunction to anything in the entire world. He had gotten turned around in that storm and let Bruiser have his lead, and wound up here. Of course, he reckoned it was a good thing, seeing how things had worked out. William was a fine strapping boy, but Chris didn't know how he would've been helping his sister come into the world.

He brought the milk and fixings into the cabin and paused to stare in the cracked mirror hanging near the door. The man staring back was a dirty scarecrow. His brown hair and beard that had long been flaked with gray, was also caked with mud.

"No wonder you scared everybody, you danged saddle-bum."

"What was that, Mr. Baker?"

"Nothing, Ma'am." He glanced at her lying on the bed. "I'm sorry I'm such a sight. It's a wonder I didn't scare that child to death, being the first thing she looked at."

Chris washed up on the porch the best he could, then made coffee. He warmed the biscuits and jerky, and fried the eggs in the cast iron skilled she had hanging on the wall. It wasn't much, but along with the milk, he guessed it to be enough for Mrs. Shafer and the boy. He sat nursing the last of the coffee as William cleaned the dishes, considering what to do next.

"I want to thank you again, Mr. Baker. You've been extremely helpful. And I'm sure my husband will be grateful as well," she said in a hushed voice.

"Much obliged for the compliment, ma'am. Is she asleep?"

"Yes. Isn't she beautiful?"

"Yes, ma'am. She certainly is. I'd like to be holding her some after she wakes up," he said with a nod. "The only time I got to hold her was when I wrapped her in that blanket."

"I might take you up on that, Mr. Baker. When she wakes, she'll probably need changing. I'll let you have her then. What would you say to that?"

"I'd be saying *thank you*. I wouldn't mind changing her a'tall."

"Really? And where did you learn so much about babies, Mr. Baker? Do you have children of your own?"

"No, ma'am. I ain't never been married either. I'm guessing no woman would have me. But you see, when you're raised the way I was, you come from a big family with a lot of brothers and sisters. And being the oldest of the lot, I had to do my share of taking care of my brothers and sisters. That is, until I got old enough to help my pappy around the farm. So, I just naturally learned how to do some of those things."

"Is that how you learned about *birthing*? I mean," she glanced away and blushed, "you did seem to know quite a lot about that, also."

"Partly. I was called on once to help my ma with my youngest sister, Viola. The pains sort of took us all by surprise. You could have shook Viola's hand by the time the neighbor woman showed up to help. And I helped deliver most of the animals around the farm. I don't reckon they're too different when it comes to giving birth. And I once happened upon a woman back during the war giving birth. She was holed up inside a house all by herself with nary a soul in sight. So, I stayed around and helped until she had delivered a fine son. Only it seemed to take her a whole lot longer to bring that Yankee into the world than what it took you with your daughter. I was beginning to think the war was gonna end by the time that boy arrived."

"Well, you've been very kind, and I'm certainly glad you were here to help."

They sat quietly just staring at each other for a long while. William finished the dishes and threw a couple of logs on the fire before Chris got the nerve to ask what he had been pondering over the cup in his hands.

"What do you reckon is keeping your husband, Mrs. Shafer? Just how far is it to this here town he went to anyway?"

"Oh, I don't know exactly, but I believe it's seven or eight miles away. The storm must have delayed him. I'm sure he'll be along any minute now."

"Yes, ma'am. I reckon you're probably right," he said with a nod. "Now, I'll tell you what I'm going to do. I'm going to take William here and go out and nose around some. That is, if you think you'll be alright here by yourself for awhile."

"I'm sure I'll be fine. But where are you going? I'm certain my husband will be anxious to meet you when he arrives."

"Oh, I don't plan on being gone more'n an hour or two. We'll probably be back long before he gets here. We just plan on having us a look-see. And, I don't know, maybe pack us something back here to cook-up for supper. I thought it might be nice to have some hot vittles waiting when your husband arrives."

She smiled as Chris draped an arm around William and headed out the door. They had left plenty of firewood stacked beside the fireplace, and banked a fire to keep them warm, so Chris reckoned them to be alright until they got back. He saddled Bruiser and with William riding behind him, they headed north toward the next rise and line of trees. There wasn't any way he knew of to say what he was feeling without hurting that boy or his mother. Of course, he could be wrong, and was hoping to God he was. But men don't just leave their women folk in a fix like that. Chris had a gnawing inside his gut.

Chapter 3

"Ever shoot a man, Mister Baker?"

"Now, what kind of a question is that? See what you've done. There goes your mama's supper. Never interrupt a feller when he's about to pull the trigger." They had ridden about a mile from the cabin before spying the elk drinking from a small creek in the bottom of a wash. He had just sighted the Winchester when William's shrill voice caused the elk to bolt away.

"I'm sorry. I just wanted to know if you've ever killed anyone."

"Well, that's a blamed silly question to ask a man in the first place," he said, shoving the gun back into the scabbard. "Especially seeing as you heard me tell your ma I was in the war."

"I guess I never thought..." he said.

"No, I guess you didn't. Now that you've had time to mull it over, what do you think? Think a man can spend most of six years stomping through the gates of hell, with folks trying to kill him, and not shoot back once in awhile?"

"No, I don't guess he can. But did you kill anyone?"

"It doesn't matter none, now does it? In the first place, I don't reckon many of us were keeping track. We were too busy trying to stay alive than to start thinking about things like that. Besides, there were so many bullets flying around, I don't think there was any way of knowing if it was your bullet that killed a man or someone else's. It's not something you'd want to go through life remembering, even if there was a way of knowing."

"I'm sorry. I was just wondering what it felt like to kill a man."

"Killing ain't something that makes you feel real good, I'll tell you that."

Chris climbed on Bruiser's back and hoisted William behind him. They followed the wash another half-mile before he brought the horse to a halt and held up a hand, telling William to keep quiet. An old elk had poked his head out of a thicket about fifty yards up-wind from where they sat. He pulled the Winchester from it's scabbard and eased the hammer back, then knelt in the damp grass behind a bush where he had a clear view of the situation. Then, it was just a matter of waiting. It wasn't long before several does and their young followed the old buck into the creek to quench their thirst. Chris sighted in on the largest of the young bucks and pulled the trigger. The rest bolted as the elk dropped where he'd taken his last drink of cool water.

"To answer your question about killing," he said, shoving the gun back into the scabbard, "I heaved my guts out after the first battle was over. So did most of the other guys who were with me. Grab Bruiser's reigns and follow me." He led the way to where the elk was lying and began the cleaning process. William stood quietly watching until he had almost finished.

"Didn't it get easier?"

"What? The killing?"

He nodded.

"Some. We quit heaving our stomachs out, if that's what you mean. But I don't know that you ever want it to get easy." Chris paused to look at him. "Fact is, when you start thinking killing a man is easy, you've gotten yourself into some real trouble."

"How's that, Mr. Baker?"

"You're just full of questions now, ain't you, boy?" he said, rinsing his knife and hands in the creek.

"My dad said he killed a man once, and it was okay, if you do it for the right reason. So, I was just wondering if it was any easier?"

"Easier than what? Killing a man for the wrong reason?"

"Yeah." He nodded.

"Well, I wouldn't really know about that now, would I? Seeing as I've never killed a man for what I believed was the wrong reason. But, I don't think it should ever get easy to kill a man for any reason. And," he paused as he hoisted the elk across Bruiser's neck in front of the saddle, "if you're ever called on to do the killing, make sure you're on the right side. Because, you're fixin' to take away the most precious gift that God gave a man, and he ain't gonna take it lightly if you're in the wrong. Understand what I'm saying, boy?"

"Yes, sir."

******

Bruiser didn't like the idea of having to carry the dead elk draped across his back, but calmed down after Chris allowed him eat his fill of the wild oats growing along the creek. William discovered a patch of wild onions not too far from where the horse was gorging himself, so Chris stuffed his belongings into one saddlebag, and the two of them dug enough of onions to fill the other bag. It was late in the afternoon when they reached the cabin, and there still wasn't any sign of Mrs. Shafer's husband. Chris took the elk to the barn to skin and cut into manageable hunks while William stoked the fire. Chris tossed a hunk of rump-roast into Mrs. Shafer's dutch oven with a fistful of onions, and hung it over the flames to cook.

After coaxing another half-gallon of milk from the cow, he turned her and Bruiser loose to eat their evening meal of fresh grass growing around the place. William came out of the house and wandered around like he was lost before deciding to join Chris mucking out the stalls.

"Worried about you pa, son?"

"Some."

"Figures. Don't blame you none. But you're probably not near as worried as your ma. If you're fixin' to fall apart, don't go doing it in front of her. You're the man of the house now. That is, until your pa shows back up, and its up to you to hold things together. Think you can handle it?"

"Yes, sir."

"Yep, I reckon you can. Come on, we'd better be checking on supper before it burns." He slapped the boy on the shoulder and headed toward the house.

******

"Reckon what day of the week this is, ma'am?" They had just finished eating and were watching Chris give Edith her first bath.

"I believe it's Friday, Mr. Baker. Why do you ask?"

"Well, I was just thinking that maybe, if you're up to it, we might head into town tomorrow and find us a place to spend the night. That way, if they've got themselves a church, we might take in the Sunday morning service. Of course, I don't have any idea where this town is, let alone if they've even got a church there."

"Yes, I do believe they have a small church. And yes, I would love to go with you, although I have no idea how you plan on getting us all there. I didn't know that you were a religious man, Mr. Baker."

"Yes, ma'am. At least I try to be. And, getting y'all there might be a little rough, seeing as you just had this here young'un. But, I kind of figured on letting y'all climb on that old horse of mine, and I'd just walk. He gets sort of ornery, and he might balk having to carry all four of us at one time."

"Walk, Mr. Baker?" She laughed and shook her head. "I'm afraid you don't know what you're letting yourself in for. Like I said, it's seven miles or more to town."

"Yes, Ma'am. You've already explained it to me once. But all us southern boys used to walk a site more than that most every day back during the war. So, I ain't a figuring it'll hurt me none to take a little stroll getting to the meeting-house. I'd actually thought about us waiting 'til Sunday morning, but I kind of figured it might be a little rough on you and the baby. Besides, I thought that while we was there, we might nose around Saturday afternoon and see if anyone knows anything as to what could have happened to your husband."

"Thank you, Mr. Baker. That is very thoughtful of you," she said softly. "To be frank, we have been rather worried."

"Yes Ma'am. I figured you might be."

"Wouldn't it be easier if you hooked your horse to our wagon, though? Then we all could ride, and you wouldn't have to walk."

"Yes, Ma'am, it might be. And the thought had crossed my mind. But if you don't mind me saying so, Ma'am, that old wagon's in pretty sorry shape. Where'd y'all get that contraption, anyway?"

"We bought it in Missouri after our prairie schooner caught fire. Why?"

"Na, you're joshing me. Y'all didn't come all the way from Missouri in that thing."

"We most certainly did." A crease appeared between her eyebrows as she set her lips into a thin line.

"Well, how long you folks been here?" Chris glanced around the room. "I know the cabin's been here a while, but I just took it for granted that y'all hadn't been here too long."

"We've been here almost a year, Mr. Baker." She began fingering a tattered piece of lace on the left sleeve of her faded blue dress as she continued in a small voice. "It's been a struggle for us, at best. First, it was losing everything we owned in the fire that took our prairie schooner. Then, after scraping together what we could, just to get here, my husband spent our life savings buying this farm." She raised her hands and let them fall to her lap with a sigh.

"It's a beautiful piece of land, Ma'am."

"Yes, but the creek and pond are only seasonal and run dry during the summer. We had no idea when we purchased the land, but there's no water for us, let alone for farming or cattle. And what few head we had seemed to vanish into thin air. So, there you have it, Mr. Baker. The saga of the Shafer family."

He excused himself, and headed to the barn. In reality, the old wagon he'd found parked in the mud had been a sorry excuse to begin with. It was half the size of a good schooner, and whoever built it had thrown it together in a hurry without much thought for comfort or how long it might last. Chris couldn't imagine anyone packing their family inside something like that, and asking them to travel halfway across the United States. But, according to this woman, her husband had. Then, from the look of things, the over-grown buckboard had been driven hard on its way West, and abandoned in the weather with no thought of trying to preserve what little good was left in its weathered boards.

Chris found an old jack and a can of grease made from a mixture of pine tar and tallow under the seat. He lit a coal-oil lamp and hung it on one of the sideboards, then tried pulling one of the wheels to give it a dose of grease.

"Dang it!" he said, as the metal rim came off and the wheel fell apart in his hands. Grumbling to himself, he left the wagon sitting on blocks and carried the lantern to the barn where he washed in a bucket of rain water. He made a bed of saddle blankets in one of the empty stalls, and satisfied himself with the thought that Bruiser wouldn't have liked being hitched to any wagon in the first place, especially one that looked as bad as the one outside. But he also knew that his horses' displeasure couldn't be compared to what Mrs. Shafer might feel when they discovered what was keeping her husband from returning home.

Chapter 4

Bruiser didn't seem to mind having a woman and her baby sitting on his back. The horse didn't even complain when Chris hoisted William up behind her either. Chris guessed it made him feel kind of important. Perhaps like the donkey Mary rode on her way to Bethlehem. Only Mary didn't have any children besides Jesus, and he wasn't born at the time. But, Chris had always figured that most women who were doing their best at being a mother were kin to Mary one way or the other.

"Sorry I ain't got no sidesaddle for you to ride on, Ma'am," he said, as she made a fuss over her dress that kept wanting to ride up around the calves of her legs no matter what she did.

"That's quite alright, Mr. Baker. I'm sure men don't have much use for a side saddle."

"No, Ma'am, we don't. Just make yourself as comfortable as possible. Me and William here promise not to stare."

"Thank you, Mr. Baker. I know you are a gentleman, but I'm afraid you've already seen more of me than my stocking legs."

Chris had never thought of himself as one to get easily embarrassed, but his face flushed as he glanced up from tying a lead rope to Bruiser's bridle to see her grinning. He felt his cheeks burn as she burst out laughing.

"That's quite alright, Mr. Baker. I understood that it was needed. But, I believe I will get down and walk beside you when we reach the outskirts of town, if you don't mind."

"No, Ma'am. That will be fine. Y'all hang on tight now," he said and started off at a brisk walk. "Ma'am?"

"Yes, Mr. Baker?"

"What ever happened to them critters that pulled that contraption y'all rode in when you came out here from Missouri?"

"My husband sold them after we purchased this place and got moved in."

"Sold them, Ma'am?" He glanced back over his shoulder.

"Yes, Mr. Baker. Sold them. All but one horse. A fine gelding named Howard. He was riding Howard when he left for town several days ago. Why do you ask?"

"Just trying to make sense of it, that's all. Why would a feller who's fixin' to build hisself a spread like you got want to go and sell all his critters before he even gets started? What was he figuring on working the land with?"

"That is something you should ask my husband, when you finally get to meet him."

"Yes, Ma'am. But I reckon it really ain't none of my business in the first place. A feller has every right to run his own spread the way he sees fit. I was just wondering, that's all."

"You recall me telling you about the fire that took our belongings in Missouri?"

He nodded.

"Well, we didn't have much when we arrived, and everything in California cost more than we expected. First, we had to purchase the ranch. The house with the land cost five dollars an acre."

"How much land you got, ma'am?"

"Close to a thousand acres, Mr. Baker."

Chris whistled, knowing that five thousand dollars wasn't a whole lot for good grass land. But ten dollars might have been a little steep for that lean-to barn and shack she kept calling a house.

"Then we had to furnish the house and buy supplies and what few animals we could find. Do you realize how scarce cattle are in California, Mr. Baker?"

"No, Ma'am. I haven't tried buying any since coming here myself."

"Well, everyone is out seeking to get rich looking for gold. No one's raising cattle around here. And when you are lucky enough to find someone who has some he'd like to sell, there's always others who have the means and are willing to pay more for the same cattle. George spent a fortune for what few head we did have. Then, between the dry summer and Indians coming out of the hills and just taking them, we seem to have lost every one of them. That's why you found us living in the condition we are in."

"Yes, Ma'am. Sorry you've had so much trouble. But, I'm glad you told me."

He walked the next mile or two in silence, leading Bruiser and mulling what he had just heard inside his head. He knew that woman was telling him what she believed was the truth. But, Chris had passed through several large cattle ranches on his way there, and every one of them had thousands of head of Spanish cattle. He knew they weren't the most desirable critters in the world, and they did have a tendency to be ornery. But, you can eat them, and they're fine for starting a herd. He didn't know if this woman had simply failed to see them, or someone had been storying to her. But what she had just told him simply wasn't true, at least to some one who knew the cattle business the way he did. Besides, Chris couldn't see any furnishings, outside that old table, chair and a couple of cots. And there certainly weren't any supplies except for that elk he had shot and left hanging in the barn.

It was around midday when they came to a place where the road forked off to the left. They could actually see the town lying in the distance where the river snaked through a bunch of trees. A little house not much bigger than the Shafer's set off the road to the right. There were a passel of children running wild out front, while a woman was busy doing her laundry in a washtub. Chris waved his hat toward them and shouted "howdy" without breaking stride. A mongrel dog came charging through the dust barking. The dog made one pass around Chris' feet and under Bruiser's legs before heading back like he'd won the battle of Gettysburg. While he hadn't bitten or harmed anyone, Bruiser didn't care to have a yapping dog around his feet, and started kicking up a fuss. He reared as if he was going to throw the woman and her children, so Chris took his hat and gave him a good whack across the nose.

"Yah!" he yelled, and jerked down on the lead rope. But the horse only glanced once, before rearing again.

"Come on, now! Quit acting like a fool!" He whacked him again, but the horse acted as if Chris wasn't even present.

"You dad-blamed excuse of a mule-headed jackass." He jerked Bruiser's head real low. Mrs. Shafer and her son quit yelling as Bruiser calmed to a snorting, stamping fit to glare at his owner. "It's a wonder you didn't throw that woman and her younguns. You idgit!"

"Yeah, I know," he added as he jammed his hat back on his head. "I didn't like him much either. Probably a dad-blamed Yankee dog. But if you ever do something like that again," he pulled his forty-four from its holster to wave it in front of Bruiser's nose, "I'm gonna blow your danged head off and cook your ornery carcass for supper. You got that, you lazy no good bag of bones?"

"Mr. Baker, please..." Mrs. Shafer panted and held the baby against her breast. "I'll admit we were frightened, but there's really no reason to threaten this horse with violence. It was the dog's fault."

"I don't plan on hurting him much, Ma'am." He shoved the gun back in its holster and gave the lead rope a tug. Bruiser snorted and glanced toward the barking dog as he started forward. "Me and this cayuse have been friends a long time. But if he keeps acting like a fool, I still might eat him for supper. You got that, you lazy no good bag of bones?"

The horse snorted and shook his head as if he were disgusted. With one more glance at the barking dog, the horse set a brisk pace that caused Chris to stretch his legs in order to keep up with him.

"He ain't a bad horse, Ma'am." Chris winked at William. "He's just set in his ways, and we need to come to a little understanding once in awhile. Besides, he's too old and tough to try to cook. Ain't that right, Bruiser?" He shook the rope and the horse nodded.

"Well, I'm certainly relieved that you were not really going to kill and eat your horse," she said after a long minute. "Sometimes it's kind of hard to know when you're serious, or when you are jesting."

"I'm sorry, Ma'am, but I reckon it's just the way I'm made. You know, the way the good Lord put me together. I think life's too full of misery as it is, and folks take things way too serious most of the time. If you can't learn to laugh at yourself and things around you once in awhile, you'll get old and die before your time."

"Yes, Mr. Baker. I suppose you're right. But I took you to be a very serious man, from the way you took over and ran things after arriving at our house."

"Well, that situation was a little different, ma'am. It was serious. Edith's a fine young lady, but I think she'd have had quite a tussle coming into the world by herself. Besides, I never said I didn't take things serious. I took most of what I seen during the war as being serious. It's just that you gotta sit back and laugh at life once in awhile, or you're gonna bust. By the way, I hope you don't mind me saying so, but I ain't never heard anyone talk the way you do, Ma'am. Except for the neighbor woman who showed up late for my sister's birthing. Heard some folks say she was a blue-blooded Yankee who married her southern husband before the war broke out. And, being the good southern-raised boy he was, he come back and joined up with us Rebs when the shooting started, even though she didn't care none for it.

"Now, don't take me wrong, I ain't saying the way you talk is bad. It's just that I ain't never heered much of it before." He glanced over his shoulder at her and William. She was one pretty woman, he had to give her that. Sitting there on top of his horse, all straight and proud, with the sunlight dancing in her chestnut hair. Chris had to wonder why a man would run off and leave her and the boy stranded by themselves.

"Well, I'm glad to know that you don't find my speech offensive, Mr. Baker," she said with a grin. "I don't find yours offensive, either. In fact, I find it rather charming."

"Reckon I never asked. But, where do y'all hail from in the first place, Ma'am?"

"Upper New York state, Mr. Baker. I guess we are what you would call real honest-to-goodness Yankees."

"Yes, Ma'am. But I ain't a gonna be holding that again' y'all. It ain't no one's fault where they are born. And I reckon God'll forgive you for being a Yankee."

"I beg your pardon?"

Her scowl vanished and she broke into laughter as he winked at William. They continued the playful banter for the next couple of miles, and Chris hated to see it end when they reached the edge of town. He helped Mrs. Shafer down and held Edith while she limped around and stretched her legs.

"I reckon that ride was a little rough on you, wasn't it, Ma'am?"

"I'm just a little sore. I'll be alright after a short rest, Mr. Baker." She smiled and reached for her baby.

"Is this the town you were telling me about? I don't see no church," he said, glancing around. Every building had Dutch Corners painted somewhere over the door. Of course, Chris thought, there weren't a whole lot of buildings, either. Outside of a few houses, he saw a butcher shop, saloon and road house that served as a combination hotel and restaurant.

"No, Hills Ferry is another two miles or so further up the road, right on the river. But, I wouldn't mind resting here for awhile, if you don't mind."

"I think that might be best. You sure you're alright? You don't look too good, Ma'am."

"Yes, I'm fine, Mr. Baker. I just need to get in out of the sun for awhile and feed Edith."

"Yes, Ma'am." He helped William down and asked him to water Bruiser and meet them inside. Then, taking Mrs. Shafer by the arm, he started toward road house, but she pulled back and turned away.

"I'm sorry, Mr. Baker. I don't know what I was thinking when I agreed to go on this little trip with you. I guess I was just excited at the prospect of finding my husband. But, William and I can't go in there with you. In fact, we should really be going back home."

"Why is that, Ma'am? Did I do something wrong?"

"No, it's not you. You've been a perfect gentleman. It's just that..." she glanced at him while her face flushed, "I haven't any money. My husband took what little we had when he went to town."

"Oh, no need to worry yourself none about that. I've got a little tucked inside my pocket. Come on inside, and let's see what kind of vittles they serve up here."

"No, I can't be letting you spend your money on us. Go on and get something to eat, and we'll wait out here in the shade."

Chris removed his hat and stepped back to glare at her a long minute.

"Well, now I can't say how them Yankees treat their women back where you come from, but I won't be holding to none of that."

"Mr. Baker, I only meant..."

"I know what you meant, and like I said, I won't be holding to it. I don't rightly care none if you eat to please yourself or not. But you got Edith to think of, and there ain't no way I'm gonna stand for William going hungry when I got the means of feeding him. Now, we're going inside, or I'm going to paddle your backside right here and now."

"You know, Mr. Baker, I believe you would actually do it, wouldn't you?" She set her lips into a thin line and glared.

"You bet I would. Now, come on." He took her by the arm and led her through the door.

******

The fare was simple, but good. Steak, beans, turnips and greens, and cornbread, washed down with hot coffee and a glass of milk for William. Ernest Voight, the German who had founded the little berg, was a butcher by trade, and while his saloon seemed to be doing a fair business, he made most of his money butchering cattle for the neighboring ranches. He'd also built a race track at the rear of the saloon, and word was he did pretty well from collecting his share of entry fees and horse-betting.

"How about spooning some of that pot-liquor on my bread," Chris said, handing William his plate.

"Huh?" The look on the boy's face reminded Chris of a calf staring at a new gate.

"Spoon some of that there pot-liquor on my cornbread," he repeated, pointing at the turnip greens. The boy continued staring.

"I'm afraid he doesn't know what *pot-liquor* is, Mr. Baker," Mrs. Shafer said with a grin. "As a matter of fact, neither do I."

"You're joshing."

"No, Mr. Baker, neither of us have any idea what you are talking about."

"Well," he said, as he spooned a healthy amount of turnip juice over his bread, "y'all's been missing out on some mighty good eating, if you don't mind me saying so. Pot-liquor's the leavings after you've done cooked up a mess of turnip and greens, or any other such good eatins. It's best spooned over a hunk of cornbread, but you can sop it up with biscuits, if that's to your liking."

"I see," she said with a grin, and went back to cutting her steak. That boy continued staring at Chris, making him wonder if there wasn't something wrong with him.

******

No one in the road house could remember seeing George Shafer, but since a hundred or more people passed through Dutch Corners on any given week, the news didn't surprise Chris any. He left Mrs. Shafer and William inside the road house while she fed Edith her dinner, and wandered over to the saloon to see if anyone knew something about her man. Fact was, no one could remember seeing him around Dutch Corners at all. He returned to the road house to find a couple of half-drunken cowboys telling Mrs. Shafer what they'd like to do with her, if they ever caught her alone.

"I wouldn't be bothering her that-a-way, if I were you," he said, leaning against the doorpost.

"And, who might you be?" The larger of the two straightened up like his size might somehow frighten Chris.

"The feller who's looking out after this woman and her children 'til her husband gets back."

"Do tell. And just what are you planning on doing, if I decide to take over your job?"

"Well, you keep talking nonsense like that, and I'll be forced to say or do something that we're both liable to be sorry for." Chris slipped the leather thong loose that held his forty-four in its holster as he stepped away from Mrs. Shafer's table. Ernest Voight ran to usher her and William toward a corner where they might be safer.

"No, I think it's you who's gonna be sorry." He cracked his knuckles and flexed his fingers. "You're gonna be coughing up blood, while me and Billy get better acquainted with this woman."

"Better quit while you're ahead, Frank." His friend tossed back the rest of his drink and scooted away from the table.

"Why's that?"

"Because, you're about to get yourself killed by Nails Baker. Of course, that might make you kinda famous 'round these parts. But," he grinned real big, "you'll still be dead."

"Na, you're lying. That ain't him." He continued eyeing Chris while shaking his head.

"No? Go ahead, if you wanna take the chance. Let's see what happens."

"Hell, he ain't worth it," he said after a long minute and kicked a chair. He started toward the door and paused to stare at Mrs. Shafer. "She ain't either." His friend laughed as he followed him outside.

"I'm sorry about all this," Ernest Voight said as he ushered Mrs. Shafer back to the table. "It doesn't happen very often." He paused to study Chris. "Who's this Nails Baker they were talking about?"

"Oh, I don't know. Just some feller who got himself a reputation for using a gun back Georgia way I heard tell."

"Are you him?" Mrs. Shafer asked. Her brown eyes reminded Chris of dark pools staring from the shadow across the table.

"Who, Nails Baker?"

"Yes. Your last name is Baker, isn't it?"

"Well, yeah, but do I look like a gunfighter to you?"

"I don't know. I've never seen one that I know of. Are you a gunfighter, Mr. Baker?"

"No, at least I've never thought of myself as one. To tell the truth, I'm from Georgia…at least I lived there awhile before the war. We Bakers originally came from Tennessee. But I don't think Nails Baker really exists." He laughed as he paid the bill. "And, if he does, I don't think you'd have anything to worry about, after seeing the way you handled your shotgun. If you and him were ever to collide, I think he'd wind-up on the short end of that switch."

Chapter 5

Hills Ferry lay in a low flat area, over-looking the San Joaquin River. It reminded Chris of the several mining towns he had passed through on his way west, with one main road leading toward the river, crowded with gold-hungry miners in a hurry to get somewhere. Hills Ferry was different though, in that it didn't have actual gold-mining taking place, outside of a few coverall-clad men scratching around in the dirt near the river. What it did have was a ferry-barge, allowing travelers and their belongings to cross the river, where they could follow the mining trail to the Mother Lode around Jamestown, Sonora and Angels Camp. It also had the advantage of a large docking area for the riverboats that made regular stops, carrying passengers and supplies from Stockston and San Francisco. On their return trips, the boats would carry wheat and other farm-grown products, along with passengers wanting to travel down river. As they entered town, Chris paused in the middle of the dusty road to stare at a large white paddle-wheeler tied at the dock. She wasn't quite as large as some of the riverboats he had seen along the Mississippi, but she was still quiet a sight, with smoke bellowing out her stacks, and people bustling about her decks. She had the name *Continental* painted in red letters across her bow.

"Remind you of home, Mr. Baker?"

"A little." He glanced down at Mrs. Shafer walking by his side. She covered Edith's face with a corner of the baby blanket and smiled. He counted two hotels, two blacksmith shops, three livery stables, three general stores, four saloons, and a number of smaller businesses as they wove their way through the crowded street. By head-count, the way he would calculate cattle, Chris reckoned there might have been close to five hundred people milling around in the open. Most of them he guessed to be ordinary folks from different places and backgrounds. Mexicans, whites, some Chinese, and a handful of blacks enjoying the freedom of California. He also guessed most of them were like everyone else, trying to scratch out a living the best they knew how.

But he also knew that a few were nothing but no-account thieves and rustlers, and he was quick to spy a few of them eyeing the woman and her baby at his side. He also knew that attractive women were scarce in California, and he'd have to stick close to Mrs. Shafer and her children until he found her husband. Then, the responsibility of caring and worrying about them would fall back on George Shafer's shoulders, and he could take Bruiser and cross the river to head up toward the Mother Lode himself, if he wanted. Not that he'd been bitten by gold-fever, he reasoned. But he still had an itch to see what lay on the other side of any mountain. The problem at that moment was, he had a woman and a couple of kids to care for who didn't belong to him, and finding George Shafer might be a problem. The truth was, he didn't know where to start. He stopped in front of the Hills Ferry Hotel and helped William down.

"We'd best be seeing about finding a couple of rooms. And no arguing out of you," he said, as Mrs. Shafer started to protest.

The man behind the desk gave them adjoining rooms on the second floor with windows that opened onto the noisy street. He left Mrs. Shafer and the baby with orders to lock their door and took William to go nosing around. It was at the third livery stable at the edge of town where William grabbed his arm and started shouting, "That's my dad's horse!"

"You sure, boy?" Chris said, studying the chestnut gelding.

"Yes, I'm sure. That's Howard."

The man who ran the livery, a short, balding fellow who walked with a limp, said the man who rode the chestnut had left him three or four days earlier, and headed down the street.

"Gave me two-bits and said he'd be coming back, but I ain't seen hide nor hair of him since."

"Well, the horse belongs to this here boy's daddy. Can you tell us what the man looked like?"

"Oh, I don't know, let's see. Average height...'round five-seven, maybe five-eight. Brown hair, if I remember right. Good-looking sort of a guy. Spoke like a Yankee, kinda like this boy does."

"Sound like your pa, son?"

William nodded as he ran a hand down the glossy coat of the horse.

"Much obliged, mister." Chris shook the grizzled paw of the stable owner.

"Ross. Tom Ross. Them that likes me calls me Reb. That's where I got myself this limp. Took a Yankee ball at Fredricksburg. You was there too, weren't you, son?"

"Yes, sir. I seen a bit of Yankee led in my day," Chris said with a nod. "A lot of good men fell at Fredricksburg, on both sides."

"You were there leading the troops." He got teary-eyed as his voice quivered, causing William to stop petting the horse to listen. "I thought I recognized you when you came in, Captain. I was in the third division, and we follered right behind you and your men second day into the battle. Shore one hell of a fight, I'll tell you that." He turned toward William as he continued talking.

"Ol' Cap here was right out in front of his men leading the charge, and we was behind 'em. Powder smoke got so thick you couldn't see ten feet in front of you, but he kept right on going, yelling and blazing away with that six-gun of his. Fellers dropping all around us. I musta climbed over a hundred good men charging the Yankee lines. It was hell, boy. But the Captain here kept us going 'till them Yanks pulled back." He turned to grin at Chris.

"You was tough as nails, Captain. Still don't know how you kept from getting shot."

"Just lucky, I guess. A lot of men did, and a lot of good men died." Chris fished around inside his pocket for a double eagle. "How much do this boy's folks owe you for the keep of this horse?"

"Oh, Captain," he held up his hand, "I can't take your money. We owe you for what you did in the war."

"You ain't taking my money, Reb. I'm simply paying a bill that's owed you, and this boy's folks are gonna pay me back. Besides," he shoved the twenty-dollar gold piece into his hand, "the war's over, and we're all just alike now. Each of us has to get along and make it the best way we know how."

******

He made a stop at the local doctor's office, asking him to make a house-call at the hotel sometime during the day to check on Mrs. Shafer and the baby. It wasn't that he hadn't birthed any babies before, but Chris had never claimed to be a doctor and somehow thought Mrs. Shafer might be kind of special. Besides, he had no idea if Yankee women were as fit giving birth as a true southern lady. They might have special needs he might not know about. Leaving the doctor's office, they entered Newman's Dry Goods Store to nose around the shelves, while asking the customers if anyone knew anything about William's pa.

"Sure, I know something about him." The man with a white apron who was stocking shelves paused to stare at them. "By the way, I'm Simon Newman." He wiped his hand on the apron before poking it out for Chris to shake. "You're…?"

"Chris," he shook the hand in a firm grip. "And this is William. We're looking for his pa. You were saying you knew something about him?"

"Yes, I do. He came in here several days ago with a list of supplies he needed. Said he'd be back later that day to pay for them, but never returned. Word is that he went over to the Gold Dust Saloon and got involved with a card game and lost his money. The last anyone saw of him, he took a job aboard the *H. E. Wright*. That's a small steamer that makes it into dock once or twice a month." He looked at William and shrugged. "Sorry, son. But your pa's gone down river, and probably won't be returning for two or three weeks."

"Much obliged," Chris said, before pulling a pretty white dress off the rack. "I'm sure Mrs. Shafer will be happy to at least know her husband's still alive and well. And, I'm sure she would like wearing this to Sunday meeting, along with that blue bonnet you've got hanging on that rack yonder."

He also bought clean shirts for himself, and a clean shirt and new coat for William, since the sleeves of the one the boy had on rode halfway up his elbows. It was getting dark by the time they returned to the hotel, and Mrs. Shafer was halfway between being relieved and cross at being abandoned inside the hotel with the baby all afternoon.

"Oh, my word," she said pulling the dress from the box. "It's beautiful. But, I can't take this, Mr. Baker. You've already spent too much money on us. Dinner at Dutch Corners and this hotel room and William's coat and shirt. I can't..." her eyes got misty as she shook her head. "You've spent all your money on us. There's no way I can ever repay you."

"Didn't ask you to. Besides, you've got no way of knowing whether I've spent all my money on you, now do you?" She shook her head. "I happen to have a little money saved, and if I want to spend it on you and the boy here, I don't see how it's gonna hurt anything. Them clothes are for going to Sunday meeting and worshiping the Creator with. It ain't like I'm acting bold toward you or nothing. Now, get washed up, whilst me and William go to our room and do the same. There's a Chinaman who's got himself an eating place down the street, and I'm a hankering to try some of his vittles."

******

"By the way," Mrs. Shafer paused with a forkful of what Chris had described as funny-looking noodles, "a very nice doctor and his wife paid Edith and me a visit in the hotel."

"Yes, Ma'am." Chris gave up trying to pick up his noodles with bamboo chopsticks like the people at the next table were doing. The fact that they were Chinese and had been doing it all their lives had seemed to escape him. "And what'd they say?"

"They said you had paid them, and asked them to examine us."

"I reckon that means the doc checked y'all out from head to toe, then?"

"Yes, it does. And, I might add, he said we are both fit as a fiddle. But you didn't have to go to all that expense and trouble. I would have told you if I thought something was wrong."

"Just making sure, Ma'am. I wouldn't want the job of explaining to your husband how come you or Edith were sick or dead."

"Mr. Baker found where Daddy is," William said, over a forkful of rice.

"Oh, is that true?"

"Yes, Ma'am. I've been aiming to tell you, but just didn't know how."

"Oh?" She dropped her fork and held a napkin to her lips. "How…how bad is it."

"Now, don't go fretting yourself none. It ain't bad like he's hurt or gotten himself dead." Chris laid a hand on her arm. "It just that...we'll he just ain't here in Hills Ferry, that's all."

"Not here? Where, then?"

"I don't rightly know, Ma'am. Well, I do, sort of, but not really."

"Maybe you can tell me, William. What is Mr. Baker trying to say? Where is your father?"

"He left on a boat that went down river."

"That's right, Ma'am. It looks as though your husband got hisself into a little jam money-wise, and took a job on one of them riverboats."

"What kind of a jam money-wise?" The frightened look on her face seem to vanish as she turned pasty-white.

"Seems after he left the horse off at the livery and ordered the supplies you folks wanted, then he went and got himself caught up into a poker game and lost his money. It's my guess that he was too embarrassed to go home and face the music. So, he got himself hired on as a hand on one of them steamers. I think the feller that runs the store called it the *H. E. Wright*, or something like that."

"I see. And do we have any idea as to how long he might be away? Are we talking months, or..." She left off by waving her hand in the air and shaking her head.

"No, Ma'am. I reckon the feller at the store said that boat pulls in here about ever three weeks or so, didn't he William?" The boy nodded and took another bite of rice.

"Thank you for all you have done, Mr. Baker. I know you didn't have to, and it was very kind of you. You are a very nice man." She stared at her plate and shook her head. "I'm sorry, but I seem to have lost my appetite."

"Reckon I can't rightly blame you none. But, you'd better at least try to eat a little more, Ma'am. You've got to be looking after your daughter now."

She smiled and began picking at her plate.

"Ma'am?" Chris said after a long minute of listening to forks scraping plates, and glasses clinking. "I know it ain't none of my affair, but does your husband have a habit of losing his money at cards?"

She hung her head like she was trying to study something on her plate. Then, Chris watched the moisture collect on her long eyelashes until a tear dropped into her noodles.

"Here, now." He reached over to dab at her eyes with his napkin. "No need for that. It was a dumb question in the first place. I have a tendency for saying dumb things. A person can probably carry on a more intelligent conversation with my horse."

"No, that's alright." She half-laughed and half-cried. "And, you would probably find out one way or the other. Yes, my husband does have a problem with gambling. But, he had promised to quit. That," she paused to take a sip of hot tea, "was our main reason for deciding to come west. *A fresh start* was what he called it. Our plan was to have our own place, grow our own food and have a roof over our heads. We actually borrowed the money from my parents to make this move. But of course, my father was dead against it for many reasons." She finished by giving a little laugh.

"And the fire inside the wagon was only part of the reason you arrived in this situation?" It was more a statement of fact than a question. She nodded, then Chris watched as she moved the noodles around the plate with her fork for a long minute.

"You guessed correctly," she said inhaling deeply. "He'd lost quite a bit of the money we had borrowed before I decided to keep it hidden."

"The rest got burned in the fire?"

"No, I had given it to the wagon master to keep. And I guess it was a good thing I did, because we wouldn't have had anything to purchase our new wagon with, if I hadn't."

They finished the meal in relative silence, and Chris saw Mrs. Shafer back to her room. He lay in the darkness of his own room, staring at the ceiling and listening to William's soft breathing in the bed next to his. He had known men and women both who had addictions. Some of them had problems with gambling, and would willingly lose their last nickel at a card table or on a roll of the dice. Others drank themselves into the poorhouse. And, he had known men who would throw away their families and reputation for one night with a woman they didn't even love or hardly knew. It seemed that Mrs. Shafer had let herself in for a lifetime of sorrow with a man who loved cards more than his own family.

On the other hand, Chris had never understood why God had saddled him with his addiction either. He couldn't stop himself from helping folks he had no business getting involved with. It was something he'd done all his life...poking his nose into places it didn't belong. And sometimes the people he was trying to help didn't even want or appreciate his help. They had returned to living the way they were before he had butted in. And here he was again. Getting involved in this woman's life, when he had no reason to be. She had a husband and family. The fact was, she had just gotten through telling him she had a mother and father somewhere back east, that evidently had some money. If he had any sense, he would let them take care of her.

But, here he was, wondering what he'd do if and when that woman's husband showed his face again. He'd more than likely think Chris had been sparking around with his wife in a way that wasn't proper, and that could lead to some real trouble. On the other hand, if he were the skunk Chris suspected he might be, he could be happy Chris had relieved him of his responsibilities as a husband and father, and take off again, saddling him with a family he didn't own, or even want. If he had any sense, he'd get up before daylight, leave enough money on the table to take care of Mrs. Shafer and her kids for a day or two, and toss his saddle across Bruiser's back. Then, he'd cross that river and see what the other side of the mountains looked like. But, laying there in the dark, Chris knew he didn't have a lick of sense. He would still be there when daylight came, looking and feeling dumber'n an old dirt clod.

Chapter 6

Sunday meeting was held on the bank of the San Joaquin River under some oak trees. The handful of worshipers sat on logs and listened as Reverend Gibson strained hard to be heard above the noise and clatter coming from the riverboat and the streets of Hills Ferry. Actually, Chris thought it wasn't a half-bad message, seeing as he talked about what folks should be doing, instead of what they shouldn't. He had always thought it senseless, even when as a young boy with patches on his knees, to keep hearing about what he'd done wrong. He'd always believed you didn't have to tell someone what it was he'd been doing wrong, because he already knew that...or at least he should. And if you didn't like what it was he had been doing, then you ought to tell him how to act. At least, that's what he figured the Good Lord did when he was alive on earth. Most of the people he met wandered around kind of lost, getting themselves into trouble because they didn't have any idea what it was they should be doing.

By the time Rev. Gibson had finished his sermon, Chris felt like he'd been talking directly to him for most of an hour. So, he decided that he just couldn't ride off and leave that woman and her two children to fend for themselves. Of course, he had no idea what he was going to do, only that he wasn't going to abandon them.

"It was so nice of you to come. I do hope you and your lovely wife and children enjoyed the service."

Chris stared at the round little woman open-mouthed for a minute.

"We ain't married, Ma'am. She ain't my wife."

"Oh?" The round woman's eyes grew large as she glanced from Mrs. Shafer to Chris and back again.

"Good morning," Mrs. Shafer said, extending her hand. "I'm Mary Shafer, and these are my children, William and Edith. Edith's only three days old." She grinned at the baby in her arms. "And Mr. Baker is a friend of ours. He's been kind enough to bring us to church and help out while my husband is away."

"Oh, I see." The round woman laughed and shook Mrs. Shafer's hand. "I'm sorry. But seeing you here together this morning…well, I just took things for granted."

"No need to apologize, Ma'am. There's worse things for a man to be accused of than being married." He shook her hand.

"The pleasure is all mine, Mr. Baker. I'm Velma Gibson. And you have been listening to my husband, Robert, this morning."

Chris shook the preacher's hand as he joined his wife's side, and told him how much he had enjoyed his talk. The conversation continued until Chris found himself seated beside Mary Ellen Shafer at Velma Gibson's table, enjoying a Sunday dinner of fried chicken, mashed potatoes and green beans grown in her back yard. It didn't take long before the question about Mrs. Shafer's husband came up.

"I…I don't really know. All I know for sure is that he took a job on a riverboat headed toward San Francisco, and will probably not be returning for two or three weeks."

The minister and his wife looked at each other for a minute, as if they was trying to read each other's minds. Mrs. Gibson who spoke first. "So what are you planning to do in the meantime, dear?"

"Go back home," Mrs. Shafer said with a weak laugh.

"Go home? You can't go back there." The words just popped out of Chris' mouth before he realized he was talking.

"And why not?" She laid the drumstick back on the plate and dabbed at her lips with a napkin.

"Because there ain't nothing there. And there's all kinds of cut-throats and what-not running around out there. You've seen it on the way here with that yahoo back at Dutch Corners. Who's gonna look after y'all?"

"I'm very capable of taking care of myself, Mr. Baker, thank you very much. You should know that by the way I welcomed you into our home."

"That's because I'm a gentleman. Ifin' I'd meant you harm, I'd of just taken that shotgun away and bopped you on the noggin, then done what I wanted to do."

"That would have been impossible, Mr. Baker. All I would have had to do was pull the trigger and sent you to see your Maker. The only reason you were able to take my gun away was because I knew you didn't mean us any harm."

"And just how did you know that? Tell me that, missy." Chris leaned close to glare in her face.

"I just knew. I have my ways of knowing."

"I doubt that." He sniggered and leaned back in his chair. "The reason I was able to take that scatter-gun away is because you was fixin' to have that young-un there. But it don't matter none, 'cause you ain't going back to that place of yours. And, that's that!" By the time he had finished, the minister and his wife were staring opened-mouth.

"And, pray tell, Mr. Baker, who is going to stop me?"

"I am, that's who. There ain't nothing out there for miles but grass and weeds. There ain't no vittles except for that elk I shot a couple of days ago. And it's probably done been ett by a pack of coyotes. You just ain't going. It's too dangerous." He finished by shaking his head.

"May I remind you, Mr. Baker, that you are not my husband. And, while I will be eternally thankful for your kindness and wonderful help, I will do what I bloody-well please." That last comment brought a gasp from the preacher's wife as Mrs. Shafer scooted her chair away from the table.

"If you will please excuse me, I think I will be returning to my hotel room. Thank you for a wonderful dinner, Mrs. Gibson. Reverend," she added with a nod. Then, grabbing her son's hand and with the baby tucked in the other arm, she headed toward the door. "Come along, William."

"But, what about Mr. Baker, Ma?" The boy glanced at the man seated at the table.

"Mr. Baker is a grown man, William. He may go where and when he pleases." She closed the door with a bang.

"Well, I guess she told me how the cow got in the cabbage patch," Chris said with a final nod.

******

He spent a tolerable time of polite talk with Reverend Gibson and tried his best explaining the situation. They agreed that Mrs. Shafer had no business being stuck by herself in the remote cabin with two small children. Reverend Gibson said he would keep an eye out for her husband, and try to talk some sense into him when he arrived back to town. His wife claimed she knew of a family living at the edge of town that had some extra room and might be happy to put the Shafer's up for a spell.

"Or," she said, glancing at her husband, "we could let them stay with us. We have an empty bedroom ourselves."

Chris thanked them and left to care for his horse at the livery. It was late in the afternoon and he found Reb mucking out one of the stalls.

"I need to have a little confab with you, Reb, about the Shafer's horse," he said, taking a seat on top of a grain barrel.

"Yeah, what about him?" Reb gave the pitchfork a toss into a stack of hay before pulling a plug of tobacco from his shirt pocket and taking a healthy bite. "Chew?" He offered Chris the plug.

"No, thanks. I was thinking I might take it back to her house for a spell, where she can't be using him."

"Yeah, and why's that?" He turned to spit in the hay.

"Seems she's got it stuck in her head that she wants to be going home, and seeing as I don't think a woman's got no business being out there all by herself..." he ended with a shrug.

"You aim to see that she's stranded, that's it?"

Chris nodded.

"Well, it ain't no never-mind to me what either one of you do, so long as someone pays the bills. And seeing as you done paid that man's bill, I reckon I might let you have his horse. Except some folks might call it stealing if you rode off with another man's animal. Now, horse-thieving's a hanging offense here same as it is any place else, so keep it in mind that if that man returns and wants his horse, he might start by calling you a horse-thief."

"Reckon I didn't consider it that way," Chris said. "That might pose as a problem."

"Yes, sir. Now, what I can do is give you back your money for that nag's keep, and hold the horse hostage until the bill is paid. Then, unless that woman's able to come up with the payment somehow, she'd have one hell of a walk getting home. It might also force her husband to look her in the eye when he gets back here in Hills Ferry."

"If he ever gets back."

"There's that too. What are you going to do if he doesn't?" Reb turn his head to spit.

"Don't know. Go down river looking for him, I reckon."

"You sure some Yankee didn't shoot you in the head," Reb said as he doubled over laughing. "You've never been to San Francisco, or Sacramento, have you son?"

Chris shook his head.

"Well, let me tell you about those places. You could lose Sherman's army in either one and not be able to find them again. Na," he shook his head, "take my advice and forget about that woman and them kids of hers. They ain't your problem in the first place. There's plenty of folks right here in this town that'll look after her. Go on," he slapped Chris on the shoulder, "have yourself a good time while you're here in Hills Ferry. Then get on that horse of yours and head somewhere else."

"You're probably right. Thanks." Chris swatted him back and headed toward the door.

"What about the money for Shafer's horse?" He yelled.

"Add it to Bruiser's keep. It won't be enough the way he eats."

That's when he noticed it sitting in a corner covered with dust and cobwebs. He knew he should have kept on going, but he just couldn't help himself.

"That old surrey belong to you?"

"Does now. Used to belong to a feller called Hoot Johnson. He died awhile back from lead poisoning. Forty-five caliber kind," he said with a nod. "Came here with big ideas of making it rich running a faro table over at the Gold Dust, only he made a mistake when he tried dealing short-handed to Joaquin Murrieta. Joaquin makes Hills Ferry his headquarters once in a while. You know that, don't you?"

Chris shook his head.

"Well, he does. So, watch yourself if you run across him. Anyway, ol' Joaquin made hisself quite a living dealing faro before he took to outlawing, so he knew it when Hoot tried to cheat him."

"How much for the surrey?"

"You interested?"

"Yeah, my ma had one just like it before the war," he said, running his fingers along the fringed top.

"Well, I don't rightly know what a feller like you would be doing with a rig like this, but let's see. How about sixty dollars for the whole lot, including them two horses that used to pull the contraption." Reb pointed to a matching pair of white-dappled horses in the corner stall.

"The rig alone is worth that," Chris said. "And those dapples are far from being dead."

"Yeah, I know the horses ain't half bad, and I might get a little more by selling them to someone who didn't know no better. But they can't be ridden, and they ain't strong enough to do no field work, 'cause all they've ever done is pull this here buggy. They're show horses, Captain. They'd be alright if you was to put 'em in a parade, because they prance real pretty, like Tennessee walkers. But like I was saying, no one around here's interested in a two-seat buggy, because there ain't no roads fit to ride on. Now, ifin' I was to wait a year or two, which is what I was planning, I might be able to sell it for what it's really worth when things get a little more civilized. But I can't. Not now. All folks are interested in is strong horses and mules, so they can go off into the hills looking for gold. The only thing those critters are doing is taking up space and eating feed without earning their keep."

"I'll tell you what," Chris said, digging into his pocket, "make sure it's clean, and the horses are fed, and I'll give you sixty-five in gold."

"You got yourself a deal, Captain," he grinned and shook his hand, "although I still think you're throwing your money away."

******

Chris had heard tales about a woman being as cold as ice, but had never understood what it meant until he met Mrs. Shafer for supper. If William had not been there, there wouldn't have been but a dozen words spoken all evening. When they had finished eating, he saw her to her room and listened while she locked the door. Chris was seated on the side of his bed, pulling his boots off, when William started laughing.

"Boy, Mom's sure mad at you, isn't she?"

"I reckon." he tossed his boots in the corner and unbuttoned his shirt.

"I guess it's because she wants to go back home and you won't let her."

"I suppose. But y'all ain't got no business being out there all alone."

"We wouldn't be."

"You wouldn't?" He stopped with his pants halfway to his knees. "Who else would be there?"

"You."

"Now, whatever gave you that idea," he asked, and plopped on the edge of the bed to finish pulling his britches off. "I can't be going back there with you folks."

"Why not?"

"Why not? Cause I ain't your daddy, and it just wouldn't look right. Look," Chris pointed a finger at him, "you're too young to understand these things now. But I can't be going back there to stay with you and your mama while your daddy's away. And, that's just the way it is."

The boy frowned and turned his back without speaking, so Chris told him he didn't care any if the whole blamed family turned their backs on him, then blew out the lamp and crawled under the covers. It wasn't but a few minutes before he could tell William was asleep by the sound of his breathing. Chris found himself envying the boy, being so innocent. Things are always so simple and uncomplicated to a child, and problems didn't seem to bother them the same as a grownup. Chris studied the cracked plaster on the ceiling well into the night before deciding what he was going to do. Reb was right. The woman and her problems didn't really concern him, and he had no business getting involved. There were plenty of people in Hills Ferry to look after them. Good folks…like the preacher and his round wife, for instance. Chris decided he would take Mrs. Shafer and her kids to breakfast in the morning, give her a couple of dollars to tide her over, then say goodbye. Then, whatever happened to them would become someone else's problem and not his.

Chapter 7

Even though it wasn't much of a walk to most any place in town, Chris got up early and hitched the team of white dabbles to the surrey and made a big deal out of taking Mrs. Shafer and William to a small eatery at the edge of town. The way people stopped to stare as they passed made him wonder if they were thinking they looked important, or maybe simply remembering the card-shark who used to own the rig. After they had finished eating, he took them for a ride downriver, away from noise and bustle of Hills Ferry, and stopped under the shade of an oak tree to talk. They sat silent for awhile, soaking up the air, while William explored the forest of oaks and cottonwoods lining the river.

"It is absolutely beautiful here. Living on our farm, I had forgotten how beautiful the river is," she said with a smile.

"Yes, Ma'am, I agree. That place of yours has its own beauty, but this is sure pretty country."

"Tell me, Mr. Baker," she shifted in the seat to study his profile, "did you really purchase this surrey and horses?"

"Yes, Ma'am, I really did. Why, what's wrong with them?"

"Nothing. It's a nice vehicle, and the horses are beautiful. But, what on earth for? This is a most unusual mode of transportation for a single man to own."

It took Chris a second or two to decipher her hundred-dollar words, so he cleared his throat a couple of times before answering.

"I guess I was getting a little homesick. My ma had a rig exactly like this one, fringe top and all. Yankees took it, along with everything else on our farm. So, when I spied it sitting all alone there in the corner of the livery, I knew I had to have it. Now that I think about it, I reckon it was kind of silly of me."

"No, I don't think it was silly at all," she placed a gloved had against his arm and studied him with watery eyes, "not if it made you think of your mother. I know I certainly miss my mother and father both. I wish I could see them right now. And I'm afraid I owe you an apology for the way I acted last night, Mr. Baker. I treated you rather coldly and rudely, after the way you've been so nice to us. I hope you find it in your heart to forgive me."

"Ain't nothing to forgive, Ma'am. You were absolutely right. I was acting like you was my wife, and you ain't. You are a grown woman with children to look out after. And you've got to do what you think is best. Now, if you want to go back to your home, that's your business, and I've got no say in the matter…no matter if I agree with you or not."

"Well," she giggled, "I was almost ready to give in and stay here in town. What brought on the big change of heart?"

"And now you're not going to stay?" Chris felt the heat rush to his head.

"Not if you're going to agree with me. Why should I stay, when I have a farm to look after?"

"Ma'am," he said, holding her cheeks between his palms and staring her in the eyes, "in case you haven't noticed, their ain't nothing on that farm of yours that needs looking out after, except maybe that old cow. And if that's a problem, I'll ride out there this afternoon and bring her into the livery and have Reb look out after her."

"That's very considerate of you, sir," she brushed his hands from her cheeks, "but there is also my house and personal belongings…"

"Begging your pardon, but you ain't got none that I seen. And you ain't going back out there by yourself. Because I ain't letting you, and that's that!"

"Ah!" She snapped around in the seat as stiff and rigid as a Georgia pine. "Take us back to the hotel. Now!"

"Yes, Ma'am." He grabbed the reigns and released the brake before remembering the boy. "William," he bellowed, "get over here now! Your mama wants to leave."

Realizing the argument was his own fault didn't seem to help his feelings. He set the Tennessee walkers into a fast trot that caused Mrs. Shafer to hold on as the buggy bumped and skipped across the ruts and chuck-holes toward Hills Ferry. William, of course, thought the ride was down-right fun, and kept asking him to go faster. Chris had to admit the request was mighty tempting. But, upon seeing the swirling water of the San Joaquin below, he thought it best to grab hold of his temper. He had almost returned to normal by the time they stopped in front of the hotel. He saw her and the baby to their room, and unlocked the door. She turned to glare as he stood in the open doorway.

"Thank you for a lovely morning, Mr. Baker. I'm sure we will be seeing each other, sooner or later." She gave the door a shove and it almost smashed Chris in the face.

"No, you'll be seeing me now." He flung the door back open.

"What do you think you are doing? I'll scream..."

"You'll cause a big ruckus over nothing, if you do. I've got me something to say, and I want the boy to hear it too."

"Okay," she said with a curt nod. "William, come here and listen to what Mr. Baker has to say." She laid Edith on the bed and stood behind her son with both hands on his shoulders. "Alright, Mr. Baker, we're ready. What is it you have to say?"

The sight of mother and son together, posing like in a picture, caused him to stare, and it took most of a minute for Chris to conjure up the courage for what he had to say.

"We are waiting, Mr. Baker."

"Yes, Ma'am. It's just that, I know I ruffled your feathers about you going back out there to stay at your place, but it was for your own good."

"I know you meant well, Mr. Baker. But I am married. And I can't be living off your generosity, or the goodness of the people in this community, no matter what my situation might be. Can't you see? I must make do with what I have, and that farm, such as it is, is all I have. So, I have to go back."

"Yes, Ma'am. And, I reckon that's one of the reasons I like you and the boy so much. If it was me in the fix you're in, I'd be feeling much the same way. And being the kind of woman you are, I reckon you might just be able to make it somehow. But, I'd feel a whole lot better knowing you was being better looked out after."

"And who, do you suppose will be doing the looking after while my husband is away? You can't. People are going to start talking, if they haven't already."

"Pastor Gibson and the fine folks right here in Hills Ferry," he said.

"Really?" She laughed real loud. "In case you didn't notice, Pastor Gibson doesn't exactly have the largest congregation of worshipers I've seen. And frankly, there aren't too many *fine folks* in this town who would enjoy taking care of an abandoned woman and her children. No, thank you, Mr. Baker. But I'll do just fine on my own."

"Sorry, but I can't be letting you do that."

"And, just how do you propose stopping me," she hissed through her clenched teeth.

"I ain't a gonna be stopping you at all. I just ain't gonna be helping you no more. I come to California with bigger things to do, and I aim to be doing some of them. So, if you're going back to that place of yours, you'd better be figuring on how you're gonna be getting there, 'cause I ain't taking you."

"I'll take Howard, my husband's horse."

"Possible. He seems tolerable enough. But that'll leave your husband stranded when he gets back into town. Won't it?"

"Perhaps, but he can manage."

"Maybe, but I still ain't taking you, and I ain't staying out at your place either. So, either you or William had better learn how to hunt, or go hungry. And you'd better learn how to milk that cow and shoot coyotes, both the four-legged and two-legged kind. 'Cause some of them that walk upright are more dangerous than them that goes around on all fours. And you'd best be thinking how you're gonna raise a garden on a patch of ground that ain't got no water when the rain stops, because I didn't see no creek or well anywheres near your place. I got no idea what y'all was figuring on drinking when summer gets here.

"And since you've got yourself a whole lot of figuring to do, I'd best leave you alone to do it. So, here," Chris fished forty dollars out of his pocket and placed it in her hand, "this is just a little something to tide you over 'till your man gets home."

"I don't want your money, or your charity," she yelled, and threw the coins at him.

"Okey-dokey," Chris said and scooped the money from the floor. "I'll just be leaving it with Pastor Gibson or the clerk downstairs in case you change your mind. Goodbye, Mrs. Shafer. William." He touched the brim of his hat and closed the door.

Chris paused outside the door, wondering if he would ever figure women out. With all her anger, and tough talk, she had given him the impression she was the one woman that might've whipped the whole Yankee army by her lonesome…except for the fact of her being a Yankee herself. Mary Ellen Shafer did sound and act mighty tough, as if she would rule the world some day, but Chris was danged if he didn't hear her crying as he headed for his room to gather his things. He almost turned back, wanting to make things right, but was able to catch himself just in the nick of time, knowing there wasn't anything to fix. The way he had left things was right. That was the way it had to be. She was George Shafer's wife, whoever and whatever he was. It was up to him to be looking after her and the kids. Edith Shafer and William were not his children, and none of his concern. And by this time tomorrow, he would be somewhere else and it'd be too late to worry about them anyway.

Chapter 8

He paid her hotel bill for the next two weeks in advance, including meals for her and William in the hotel dining room. He also gave the clerk orders to keep an eye out after them, and said he would be coming back and settle up with him when he got into town. Then, throwing his grip on Bruiser, he headed toward the river, stopping at the parson's long enough to say what needed saying. They agreed to look after Mrs. Shafer for him while he was gone. That would have made Chris feel good, except for the way they worded it. Fact was, she wasn't Chris' to be looking after, so there wasn't really any need for them to be telling him that way. Besides, he had never told them he would be coming back in the first place. He might have said it to the hotel clerk, but he didn't say it to Mrs. Shafer or the parson either one, so there wasn't any reason for the parson or his wife to act like Mrs. Shafer was his responsibility…because she wasn't. And Chris was getting tired of folks thinking she was.

He asked the man at the ferry where the river let out to, and was told it merged with several other rivers and dumped into a delta somewhere around Stockton. He also told Chris if he followed the delta long enough, he'd wind up at the Pacific Ocean. Well, that suited Chris fine, seeing as he had a hankering to see something he had never seen. He turned Bruiser and wandered downstream, following the river the rest of the day. Come nightfall, it looked about the same, except there wasn't any town in sight. He made camp and bedded down under some trees right on the bank. Chris thought it was nice and peaceful, listening to the gurgling of

Poverty Flat

the water and other sounds a fellow can hear when he's alone. The stars were so bright and clear, they looked as if he might be able to reach up toward heaven and stir them with his finger. But for all the peace and beauty, he was hanged if he didn't start thinking things he had no business thinking about. He lay rolled up in his blankets, wondering about the danged woman back in Hills Ferry. It wasn't that he was worried about anything bad happening to her. It was worse. He found himself wondering about little things, like what her and William had eaten for supper, and what they did afterward. And what they might've talked about. When he finally fell asleep sometime in the early morning, he woke thinking he'd heard her laughing. The laughter turned out to be a squirrel fussing at Bruiser from somewhere up in the tree.

"Dad-gum woman," he said, stumbling to his feet. "Remind me next time we run across some pitiful female critter like that, just to shoot 'em and get it over with."

He took his time following the river, stopping at several small settlements along the way such as Crows Landing, Mahoney's Landing and Carpenters Ferry. All of them looked pretty much the same to Chris. Mahoney's might have been a little larger than the others, having some twenty-five buildings that looked as if they were thrown together in a hurry. But all of them seemed to be doing pretty much the same thing, so Chris chose to make camp out in the open again, away from the bustle and noise of folks crowded together at the river settlements. He knew he had a passel of thinking to do, and needed the quiet to get it done. As it turned out, he didn't get a chance to do any thinking, and didn't find much quiet either. The good part was not having to think about Mrs. Shafer. He had to shoot a grizzly bear that came into camp looking to make Bruiser his evening's meal.

Shooting the grizzly meant he had to spend most of the night skinning and cleaning. Chris had shot, cleaned and skinned smaller bears back home, but found cleaning a grizzly no small matter, especially by himself. His first task was to make sure he was dead, and not playing possum. He remembered a boyhood friend named Lim Truit, who had tried cleaning a possum-playing bear once. That critter almost tore him apart before Chris and Lim's brother, Harry, pumped more lead into him. Lim was laid up inside his cabin almost two months licking his wounds.

After Chris had made sure the bear was truly dead, he hooked his rope around one of his legs and used Bruiser to roll him back and forth, while peeling his hide back with his hunting knife. Bruiser didn't like the smell of blood, and liked the smell of bear even less, and began to protest being tied to the dead creature lying on the ground.

"You think I like it any better'n you do?" Chris growled at the horse. "Remember, it was you this old grizzly came here looking to eat, not me. I kilt him to save your ornery hide, so quit acting the fool and help me get him skinned."

Chris finally had the hide hung from a tree limb, and most of the meat cut into manageable hunks by the time the sun came up. He was busy washing in the river when what looked like a hunting party made up of four Indians walked into camp. Not knowing if they were friendly or not, and seeing as his pistol and rifle were lying about ten feet away under the tree, he just grinned real big and said, "howdy."

The youngest of the hunting party grinned back and said, "hello. Nice bear." He gestured toward the hide.

"You speak English," Chris said, reaching for his shirt.

"So do you," he said with a nod.

"I deserved that. I'm Chris Baker," he said, offering his hand.

"My name is Koo-nance, but you may call me Johnny Garcia." He shook Chris' hand. The older one of the group said something in his native language while pointing with his lance toward the hide and pile of meat Chris had laid out on a tarpaulin.

"My father wants to know where the others in your hunting party are, and why they left you to do all the work."

"Ain't none," Chris said, strapping on his gunbelt. "I'm all there is."

He turned to interpret and by the looks Chris received, and hurried conversation, he knew he'd better walk lightly. Chris had known quite a bit about Indians back home, and had hunted and ate and fought with a number of them. But he didn't know much about California Indians, and if this group wanted to squabble over the grizzly, he was more than willing to let them have it. He tossed a few more sticks on the campfire and poked a hunk of bear meat on the sharp end of another stick and held it over the fire.

"Y'all hungry? I'll cook us up a hunk of this bear for breakfast, if ya want."

"No, thank you. Yokuts don't believe in eating grizzly bears," Johnny Garcia said, and squatted on his heels beside the fire.

"Well, I can't say as it's the best eating around. Kind of fatty for my taste. But, seeing as he wandered in here and spoiled a good night's sleep, I figure on having him for breakfast. Y'all are welcome to join me, if ya want."

"Eating the flesh of a grizzly is against our beliefs. There are some who believe the shaman can actually turn into the bear while doing the wa-dom buh-yee."

"What the heck is that?" he said.

"The dance of the grizzly bear. It is a dance to celebrate the spirit of the bear. Sort of a prayer that we may live in harmony with the bear, and he will treat us kindly."

"And you think your shaman, or medicine man, can actually turn into a bear while performin' this ceremony?" Chris stared at the hunk of bear meat roasting over the fire.

"Some do. They're afraid they might be eating the flesh of a human, if they eat the flesh of the grizzly."

"Boy oh boy," Chris said, pushing his hat back on his head. He stared at the boy real hard before saying, "I shore am sorry if I offended you folks. I didn't know. Honest."

Johnny turned to the others in the hunting party and conversed in Yokut a minute or two before returning to squat by the fire.

"My father says you have not offended anyone. And he is grateful that you are sorry for killing the bear, but he realizes that it is necessary once in awhile for one's safety."

"That's how it was. Mr. Bear come in here looking to eat my horse. And, seeing as I didn't think he'd let me toss a saddle across his back and ride him down river, I decided to shoot him and keep my horse instead." Johnny chuckled and shared Chris' comment with the others.

"My father says he would like to trade with you for the bear's skin."

"I'll tell you what, son. You tell your daddy he can have it for a gift. I ain't got no use for it, and I'd just have to haul it with me wherever I go. So, if he thinks it's worth something, and it's important to him, he can just have it."

One thing Chris had learned to appreciate about Indians, and found it held true with most, regardless of tribe, was that they didn't waste time with words that didn't mean much, and they didn't waste time doing things that didn't matter. It only took them a few seconds to say "much obliged," before they had the bear hide rolled and packed off through the brush on top of their shoulders. Chris grinned as he continued roasting the hunk of bear meat, knowing that toting a green hide wasn't a small feat, by anyone's imagination. The grizzly hide was as heavy as a fresh buffalo skin, and he had never liked toting one of them either. There wasn't any way he was going to cry as he watched them carting it off. He sat under the tree most of the morning with the intention of smoking enough bear meat to last until he got to the next town. Little did he know he'd ride into Graysonville late that afternoon.

******

Graysonville was quite something compared to the other places he'd seen since leaving Hills Ferry. He counted five saloons, a livery stable, two restaurants, a butcher shop, Grange hall, temperance lodge, warehouse, and two large merchandising stores. They even had a school house with a nice-looking school teacher. She was busy organizing her students into a game in the schoolyard as Chris passed. He tipped his hat and received a smile in return. A large, Victorian house with freshly painted trim, separated from the rest of the buildings caused him to stop and stare.

"Yes sir, I know what place you're talkin' about," the burly man at the livery said when Chris asked about the house. "It belongs to John Westley Van Bencroten, one of the town's founding fathers. John's one of the few fellers who came to California with a pile of money, and built that house with lumber he had shipped from back east all the way around Cape Horn. It's something to look at, ain't it? One of the prettiest houses I've ever seen."

"Yes, it sure is. But don't you think it looks kinda pretentious sitting there by its self, when most of the other houses are either tents or little clapboard buildings thrown up in a hurry," Chris said as he paid for Bruiser's keep.

"Some, but it's sure pretty."

Graysonville impressed Chris as being a full-blown boomtown, and he said as much as he ordered a cup of coffee at the restaurant closest to the river.

"Yes, it sure is," the man behind to counter said with a laugh, refilling Chris's mug. "Most everyone who comes here's been bitten by gold fever." He leaned across the counter to stare Chris in the eye. "Only thing is, the ones who are really getting rich is men like Vernon...the man running the ferry," he added with a nod toward the window.

Chris glanced through the glass to spy the heavily-loaded barge making its way across the San Joaquin River.

"I heard he's taken in some $3,500 in the past eleven days." He finished with a nod as he poured himself a mug.

"Hmm," Chris said, taking a sip from the steaming mug. "Seems like a better way to make money than trapsing up into the hills looking for gold."

"I couldn't agree with you more, sonny," he said with a grin, and poured a fresh mug for the man seated next to Chris. "That's why you see me running this place. I might work long, hot, sweaty hours, but I got me a roof over my head, food in my belly, money in my pocket, and a good wife at home. Most of them up in the hills ain't got none of that. They're only hoping to strike it rich, and few of them ever will. What are you looking to do? You don't strike me like someone who's been bitten by the fever. Are you?"

"Me? Na," Chris said, taking another sip. "At least, not that kind. I got me a bad case of tumbleweed fever, and was looking to see what lay over the next hill. Then, maybe after I've seen all I want to see, I might buy me a little spread somewhere and raise cattle."

"Good idea. There's always money in cattle, if a fellow does it right. But if you're going to see what's over those mountains, you'd better do it in a hurry." He shook his head as he slid a plate of beef and beans in front of Chris. "It gets mighty cold up there. And there ain't a winter, since coming to California, that I don't hear about some poor feller getting hisself caught out in a snowstorm and freezing to death."

Chris finished his meal and wandered up and down the streets looking things over. Nothing seemed to strike him as something he hadn't seen before, so sunset found him seated on a barrel at the dock staring at the ferry, and the hills that lay in the distance.

Chapter 9

"In a big hurry to find them nuggets?" Vernon, the ferryman, gave Chris a toothless grin as he pulled away from the dock. The sun was just starting to turn the eastern sky pink and there was a little bite in the air, as the current of the San Joaquin began tugging at the hull.

"Nope. Just wanting to go have me a look-see," Chris said, glancing back over his shoulder. Someone was yelling and trying to run while dragging a stubborn mule toward the dock. Several others had already gathered, waiting for the ferry to return.

"Well, you're the first I ever heard say that, boy. The way you were waiting when I got here this morning, I just figured you were in a hurry to get to the hills and look for gold."

"You figured wrong. I'm used to getting up early and getting things done. And I ain't got me no hankering to go getting myself wet looking through ten tons of rock to find one ounce of gold."

"You're smarter'n most of 'em that comes through here. I'll give you that," he said with a hearty laugh. He kept on talking as he took his time tying up to the opposite side of the river.

"If you're not looking for gold, what are you planning on? There's plenty of work right here in Graysonville, if you've got a head on your shoulders."

"Don't know. I ain't quite settled on that yet." Chris led Bruiser up on the bank and slid into the saddle.

"Well, if you ever decide to settle 'round here, look me up first. I've been needing someone awful fierce who ain't gonna be running off looking for gold every time someone makes a new strike."

"Much obliged. I might take you up on that."

He turned Bruiser and set off at a gentle lope, following the road. Traveling light, like he was, he overtook several Mexican freighters driving wagons and mule teams heading toward the gold fields. They seemed to be a friendly lot, waving and shouting greetings as he passed. He stopped around midday under the shade of some oaks lining the banks of the Tuolumne River, and made coffee. A group of three freighters pulled their wagon under a tree next to his, and began making camp. Chris hollered and waved them over to share his fire and opened a pack of smoked bear meat.

"Gracias," one of them said, squatting on his heels next to the fire. "My name is Julio."

"I'm Chris," he said, offering his hand.

"That's my brother, Jesus, watering the mules. This one is my cousin Paco," he said as the third man in the group joined the warmth of the fire. "He's the one you've got to watch. He will steal your woman while you are watching."

"Well, that might be kinda difficult, seeing as I ain't got one to steal," Chris said. "Coffee's ready. Help yourself."

"Gracias," Paco said. He pulled several tin mugs from a sack and reached for the pot. "Don't listen to them. They're just jealous because I married a beautiful woman, and they're still chasing the putas in the cantina." He pushed back a finely tooled sombrero and gave a full smile, showing a set of white teeth. He was a handsome young man with fine features and glossy black hair that hung to his collar. His looks were enough to fool most anyone, except for the forty-four on his hip and the brush-knife tucked inside his boot.

"Ever get much use for that hog-leg, son?" Chris said over the rim of his mug.

"A little." He frowned and studied the liquid inside his cup.

"Paco is a *pistolero*, and rode for *Doña* Garcia," Julio said. "He still works at her rancho, but has agreed to come to help us after our older brother, Roberto, got shot." He said so matter-of-factly, it took Chris a minute to collect the full impact.

"Shot? Who'd want to shoot one of you boys?"

"A lot of people," Jesus said as he joined them. "We carry supplies for the mining towns, and there are a lot of hungry people roaming the hills."

"*Si*, but the ones who shot Roberto were real *banditos*, who knew what they were doing. They shot Roberto because he had a gun and resisted. Then, they took only what they thought was valuable and rode away. He is lucky to be alive."

"How many of them were there?" Chris took another sip.

"Four. And two of them had shotguns," Jesus said.

"They didn't use a scatter-gun on your brother, did they?"

"No. But he almost died, just the same."

Chris eyed Paco a long minute as he warmed tortillas over the fire in one cast-iron skillet, and simmered beans in another.

"You man enough to face four armed men by your lonesome, boy?"

He only shrugged and kept heating the tortillas.

"Yeah, I suppose you are, if need be. Help yourselves to some bear meat, while you're at it," he said, turning the stick holding the hunks of meat. "It ain't much, but it's all I got to offer, besides the coffee. This feller cost me a whole night's sleep, and I aim to enjoy every ounce before I'm done."

Chris decided to ride along with the freighters for awhile longer in order to share their company. Any one of the three could sing as well as the next, and their music and laughter kept him from thinking about things he shouldn't. They made camp late that afternoon among a bunch of rough boulders and rocks that Jesus said had come from a volcano millions of years ago. Chris said they might of come from inside a volcano, but seeing as the good Lord didn't make the earth that long ago, they couldn't be millions of years old. The statement started a debate that only ended when Paco hollered that supper was ready.

Chris had just dished up a plate of bear meat, beans and tortillas, when six men on horseback stopped just outside their campsite. Two of them happened to be the same two that were bothering Mrs. Shafer at Dutch Corners.

"Well, well. Look who we got here, Billy." The one called Frank leaned forward in his saddle and grinned. "I still say he ain't Nails Baker. Nails Baker would be back in town with a couple of women on his arm, instead of sitting around a campfire with a bunch of Mexicans."

"He had a woman and a couple of kids last time we seen him. Maybe she's run him off," Billy said with a laugh.

"That right, Nails? She run you off?"

"Still looking to get your head split open, boy?" Chris said while spooning another pile of beans into his mouth.

Frank lost his grin and started from his saddle before a tall handsome gent, who seemed to be in charge, urged his horse between them.

"Sergeant, mind your manners."

He took his time settling back into the saddle as the leader got off his horse and removed his hat before walking over to where Chris was seated on one of Paco's rocks.

"Mind if we join you gentlemen?" he said rather polite-like.

"Better ask them folks," Chris said over a mouthful of beans. "It's their campfire. I'm just along for the ride."

"My apologies, gentlemen." He bowed his head toward the *vaqueros*. "Would it be possible for me and my companions to rest beside your campfire this evening? We have more than enough provisions for ourselves, and are willing to share what we have with you, if you wish."

The *vaqueros* glanced at each other.

"You'll have to excuse Sergeant Sorenson's rudeness. He seems to have had some run-in with Captain Baker previous to our arriving. We are quite harmless, I assure you. But, if you wish, we shall move on. My only thought was that it is getting late, and the protection of your campfire did look inviting."

The men jabbered back and forth a minute before Julio said, "*Si*, you may join us. Your men can put their horses over there," he pointed toward the opposite side of the camp from his own animals, "and you can make your beds anywhere you wish."

"Thank you very much. By the way, I am Captain Rufus Ingram of the Confederate States of America," he held out his hand toward Julio, "at your service."

He shook everyone's hand, including Chris', and turned to bark orders toward his men. Chris studied the men hard as he chewed a mouthful of bear meat. It took him a minute, seeing as there seemed to be a whole passel of folks wanting to give themselves a title such as captain or colonel during the war. But, the last thing Chris expected was someone willing to call himself a captain of the Confederate Army, way out in California after the war. By the time Captain Rufus Ingram had returned to the campfire Chris had him placed. He took a healthy swig of coffee as he sat down on a rock next to the one Chris was seated on.

"It's great luck, my finding you here, Captain Baker," he said, as Chris took another bite of beans. "Perhaps you don't remember me."

"Yeah, I remember you alright, Captain," he said, and took another sip of coffee. "Last I remembered hearing, you was off riding with Bill Quantrill in Missouri. I kinda figured you might have gotten yourself killed."

"Not hardly. I must agree that hard times fell on most of the company, but many of us survived to fight for the cause."

"In case you might've forgotten, the war's over with, Captain," he said with a snigger. "The north won, and there ain't no cause to fight for anymore."

"There are those who believe General Lee made a mistake in surrendering at Appomattox. For many of us, the war never ended. We plan to keep on fighting, and were hoping you would join us."

"Join what?" It was all Chris could do to keep from laughing. But he knew Ingram was dead serious, and so were the men riding with him. Chris glanced at Paco on the other side of the campfire, and the vaquero shrugged.

"The Knights of the Golden Circle. Look," he said in earnest, "there are sixteen thousand southern boys just like you and me right here in California. And we don't like the idea of having to give up our land and our ways to a bunch of Yankees. We're willing to keep on fighting no matter what the cost."

"Fighting for what? I don't know how long it's been since you've been back home, but there ain't nothing to fight for. They even took that little piece of bottom land my folks owned, and gave it to a bunch of carpetbagger-loving darkies. There ain't no South, Captain, not like we once knew. And there's nothing you or I can do about it."

"I beg to disagree with you, Captain Baker. There's a lot we can do. And once our fellow southerners learn of our successes, they'll once again raise up arms and take back what's rightfully theirs."

"Okay, I ain't a gonna argue with you none. Maybe you're right, and I'm just tuckered-out from ducking Yankee lead. So, tell me, Captain Ingram, what are you and this bunch planning to do besides getting yer heads blown off?"

His eyes darted around the campfire at the Mexicans busy eating their dinner before answering.

"Perhaps discussing our plans is something that should be kept private."

"Okey-dokey," Chris said, laying his tin plate aside. "Let's me and you take a little walk." He took his cup of coffee and wandered toward the river with Captain Rufus Ingram of the Confederate States of America in tow. Chris found a spot on a fallen tree at the edge of the water and took a seat. A large-mouthed bass jumped near where they were seated, making Chris wish he had a cane pole and a can full of wiggly-worms, instead of a crazy man hoping to keep a war going.

"What we plan on doing, Captain Baker, is to hold up a couple of stages carrying Yankee gold to finance our venture." He got close enough for Chris to smell the stale rum on his breath. "Plus, we already have a crew ready to sail out of San Francisco on the *Chapman*. Anyone who sees her is going to think it's only a cargo ship, but we have her armed with cannons, and every man on board is armed and dedicated to our cause."

"Ya gonna take on the whole Yankee navy with one ship?"

"No. We're going to sail toward Mexico, and waylay the first three eastbound Pacific Mail steamers we see. Everyone of them leaving San Francisco is laden with gold and silver. Then, we plan to circle the Horn and deliver it to the men of The Confederacy waiting down south. So, you can see, Captain Baker, that we are not just a few crazed men wanting to perpetuate a lost cause."

"Yeah, I'll grant that you sound mighty organized. But, then what? You got your gold from the stages and from pirating the ships. What are you gonna do with it?"

"Supply an army, Captain. And that's where you come in."

"Really?"

"Yes. We need well trained men...a lot of them. We have any number of men willing to take up the arms our gold will buy. But we need leaders, who will train and lead them into battle."

"Mighty interesting talk," Chris paused to take a sip of tepid coffee, "but the Yankees might have something to say about it, if you start invading the north, no matter how big your army is."

"Oh, but that's the twist. We've already thought about that. We don't want to invade the north...not right away."

"Then, what's the point?"

"We plan to invade Mexico."

"You what?" Chris choked on a mouthful of coffee and had to cough.

"Invade Mexico. You see, no one will be expecting it, especially the Mexican government. Our plan is to conquer Mexico. It will be easy to establish slavery there, seeing as they already have it in one form or another. Then, we will annex it into the Union as a new slave state."

It took a long minute for Chris to decide that the man was indeed both sober and serious. Then, he couldn't help himself any longer and burst out laughing.

"I'm sorry you feel that way, Captain. I can see that I wasted both your time and mine."

"You sure did, if you thought I'd go in with you on such a deal. There's a couple of things wrong with your planning," Chris said as Ingram turned to leave.

"I don't think so. We've gone over every detail carefully, time and time again."

"Well, you forgot something. First, they hang folks in California for sticking up stagecoaches. And, last time I checked, they were still hanging folks for piracy. And, seeing as the Yankee government said they're against slavery, you'll play hob talking them into annexing Mexico into the Union, even if this fool-hardy plan of yours did succeed. But, most of all, I'd have to think that Maximilian and the Mexican army might have something to say about you taking over their country. They take things like that kind of seriously down there. And, if you think I'm just being overly cautious, try asking them folks buried at the Alamo."

Rufus Ingram spun on his heel and stomped toward the camp, leaving Chris to finish his lukewarm coffee. They were gone when he returned to camp.

"What did you say to the crazy *gringo*, Señor? He was plenty angry and made all of them leave." Jesus grinned as he poured Chris a fresh mug of coffee.

Chris shared Captain Ingram's plans as best as he could. The *vaqueros* began a whooping and laughing fit before he was halfway through explaining the plan. Jesus said he wished there was some way of following them around to watch the crazy *gringos* try something that stupid. Chris might have agreed, except he had already seen enough crazy fools killed on both sides during the war. They finished eating and checked on the wagon and animals once more before bedding down by the fire. He had just about dozed off when Paco nudged him with the end of a stick.

"Hey, Chris."

"Huh?" He raised up on one elbow and reached for his gun before realizing the man wanted to talk.

"That *gringo* on the horse said you had a woman. What are you doing out here, man?"

"Na, he was mistaken. She ain't my woman," Chris said, laying back against the saddle. He studied the stars as he explained about Mrs. Shafer and her children and about the run-in he'd had with Sorenson at Dutch Corners. The vaquero was quiet when he had finished, and thinking he might have fallen asleep, Chris rolled over and closed his own eyes before hearing Paco heave a sigh.

"And you left her and her children alone?"

"They weren't my responsibility."

"No, you are wrong, *señor*. I think that *Jesus Christo* put that woman in your care, whether you like it or not."

Chris raised up to stare at him. "I just told you that she's a married woman. She's got herself a husband out running 'round somewhere. And I ain't gonna be hanging around fixing to get myself shot when her husband gets home."

Paco chuckled and shook his head.

"You lie, *señor*. A man like you doesn't worry about a jealous *hombre* with a gun. What are you really afraid of. Is she ugly?"

"Naw. In fact, she's right pretty. But, like I done said, she's married. And I ain't for hanging 'round no married woman, no matter how good-looking she is, because a feller can get to thinking thoughts he shouldn't, when he allows himself to get corralled in a situation like that."

"Ah." He nodded and rolled over to stare at Chris. "She may have been married once, but a man does not run off and leave his family. I don't think this one is coming back." He shook his head slowly. "No, I have a feeling about this one, like I did when I first saw my Aurie. I was a man of many sorrows, *Señor* Chris. The ones who hurt *Doña* Garcia also killed my Lupe. I thought I would never love another woman."

"I'm sorry."

"*Gracias*. But then I met Aurie. I knew that she was the one I was going to marry when I first saw her. Down here," he thumped his chest. "It is the same feeling I have for you, *señor*. There is nothing you can do about it, and there is nothing out here for you. Go back to her."

"Aw, you're crazier than my Aunt Hattie," he said, pulling the blanket over his shoulders.

"You'll see, *Señor* Chris. You'll see."

Chapter 10

The *vaqueros* needled Chris all the way into Jamestown about how they figured Mrs. Shafer and her kids were his to care for. The angrier he grew, the worse their needling got. He considered a time or two of whipping the lot of them, but on further consideration, decided he might not be able to handle all three at one time. So instead, he said nothing most of the way, which didn't seem to make any difference to the Mexicans, as their jesting continued.

Chris left them to off-load supplies at the general store, while he wandered down the street to do some nosing around. It was while getting a shave at the barber shop that he overheard a fat gentleman, waiting his turn in a chair against the wall, saying something about a ship out of San Francisco called the *Chapman*. Chris grabbed the barber's wrist and held the razor still as he rose to stare at the man.

"What's that you were saying about the *Chapman*?"

"I was just saying that a bunch of crazy rebs were trying to overthrow the government. They had turned it into a makeshift battleship, and planned on using it to attack the mail steamers leaving San Francisco, but their navigator lost his nerve and turned them in. The whole bunch were arrested before they got out of the harbor. Why, do you know them?"

"Na," he leaned back laughing, "I run across some feller back yonder who claimed he knew me during the war. He had the silly notion I might want to join up with them because I'm a southerner. I listened, but it was the craziest plan I'd ever heard of, and I told him so. I didn't want no part of it."

"Lucky for you," his barber said.

"Na, luck ain't got nothing to do with it. You just gotta be dumber'n a bucket of mud to start off on a fool mission like that, thinking you're gonna succeed. Besides," he added, closing his eyes, "the war's over with. The south lost, and I ain't for holding no grudges one way or the other."

The *vaqueros* had unloaded half the wagon by the time Chris returned, and were busy strapping the tarp down.

"The rest are for Sonora and Angel's Camp," Julio said when Chris asked about the remaining goods.

"Well, how about us getting some vittles at that small cantina we passed coming into town when you get finished? I'll buy." The Mexicans finished tying off the load in what Chris thought was record time. They were about to seat themselves inside the cantina when Rufus Ingram walked in and made himself welcome at their table.

"I wish you would reconsider my proposition to join us, Captain Baker."

"Well, that'd be a fine how-do, seeing as I've already heard about the *Chapman*. And, I ain't about to get myself kilt on account of you wanting to keep a war with some Yankees alive."

"I'm sorry you feel that way. I was thinking you, of all people, would understand and feel a little different, seeing as your family lost everything."

"Yes sir," Chris said with a nod as he filled their cups with coffee. "And seeing as how I'm the last Baker alive, I plan on keeping it that way."

Ingram exhaled loudly as he scooted his chair away from the table and stormed out the door amid the hoots and howls of the *vaqueros*. Chris joined in their laughter, and spilled his coffee as they tried guessing how Ingram and his men might pan out with the rest of their plans. It was over the third cup of coffee that he told them he had decided to return to Hills Ferry.

******

It took most of two days reaching Hills Ferry, and Chris decided it looked pretty much the same as when he'd left. He missed the music and laughter of the *vaqueros*, but knew they were capable of handling most anything they might run into, and really didn't need his help. He also figured that Paco was right about it being his responsibility to find out what happened to Mrs. Shafer's husband. After all, he was the one that rode up to her house during that storm and helped deliver her baby. So, Chris decided the Good Lord had given him the responsibility one way or the other. And, if it turned out that her husband had gotten himself killed, or had just run off and didn't want the responsibility of a family, then it would be up to her to decide what they were going to do. The one thing Chris had not calculated on, was that she might try doing something foolish while he was away. He stood in the middle of Ross' Livery staring at the empty spot where his buggy and Tennessee walkers should have been as the reality sunk in.

"That lady took them yesterday. I figured she'd have been back by now," Reb said matter-of-factly.

"What lady? Mrs. Shafer?"

"Yes sir. And she had the baby and little boy with her."

"Why'd you let her go?" Chris yelled, and Reb turned away to spit before giving him a go-to-blazes look.

"She said she wanted to go for a little ride, and had your permission to use the rig. And seeing how you two was all friendly with each other before you took off, I had no reason to question her."

"Got any idea where she might've gone?" Chris said somewhat quieter.

"Nope…never asked. Didn't think it was any of my business."

"Well, dagnabit, Reb! Next time she comes asking for something like that, find out, or don't go letting her take off by herself. That woman's crazy and liable to try anything."

"Well, she weren't by herself. She had that boy with her," he said, as Chris hoisted himself onto Bruiser's back. "Besides, what trouble can she get into taking a little ride?"

"You said yourself she should have been back yesterday. Besides," he turned Bruiser to leave, "she's a Yankee. That should explain everything."

"Yep, never thought of it that way," Reb yelled after Chris as he galloped down the street.

******

He had gone only three miles past Dutch Corners before running into the posse. The men looked exhausted, and were resting under a clump of cottonwoods. The big man wearing the star on his vest introduced himself as Tom Cunningham, sheriff of San Joaquin County, and offered Chris a cup of coffee.

"Thanks, but I'm in kind of a hurry to reach the Shafer place. I've been gone a few days, and that crazy woman can cause more trouble than a tow sack full of cats."

"I've known a few people like that myself," the sheriff said with a chuckle. "Mainly, I'd like to know if you've seen a short stocky feller with sandy hair by the name of Richard Collings.

"I've seen lots of fellers the last couple of days up towards Jamestown way," Chris said with a nod, "but I don't recollect hearing of anyone called by that name."

"Well, this man wouldn't have been up that way. We've chased him clean across the county line, and expect he's holed-up somewhere around these parts," Sheriff Cunningham said.

"Can't say as I can help you then. I just left Hills Ferry, and I ain't seen anyone fitting that description. If you don't mind me asking, why y'all looking for him?"

"He killed a man named John Sheldon. A friend of his, supposedly. They were drinking and got into some argument, and Collings took a knife to him."

"It appears he ain't the type of friend a feller really needs to be hanging around with. I'll keep my eyes and ears peeled," Chris said, and turned Bruiser back onto the trail.

It was almost dark when he reached the Shafer's and spied the brown horse tied to the porch. He stopped Bruiser behind the barn and slid the Winchester from the scabbard, then crept to the front door. He could hear them talking as he eased the hammer back and kicked the door open. Mrs. Shafer screamed as the man perched atop the wooden box grabbed for his gun. He froze as Chris shoved the rifle barrel against his head, then dropped the plateful of beans and cornbread he had been holding on the table with a clatter.

"That's right. Take it out nice and easy now," Chris said and he eased the pistol from it's holster. "Now, lay it on the table." He obeyed, as Mrs. Shafer seemed to explode.

"Mr. Baker! What in the world do you think you're doing, bursting into my house and pointing guns at people? Mr. Collings happens to be my guest. Put that gun away this instant!"

"Yes Ma'am." he backed away but kept the rifle pointed at Collings chest. "Now, why don't you just slide that hog-leg across the table to William there real careful like. And no funny business," he added as Collings reached for the gun, "because I ain't likely to miss at this distance."

"Mr. Baker…" Mrs. Shafer started but he waved her off.

"Excuse me, Ma'am, but I don't suppose this yahoo told you about the feller he kilt, and the posse out looking fer him, did he?"

"No, I…I…" she stuttered as her eyes darted between the two men.

"Didn't think so. I'll tell you what, sonny. Seeing as I ain't in no mood for splattering your brains all over this lady's kitchen, I'll be giving you a head start up the road before I tell that sheriff and the half-dozen fellers where you're headed."

"Easy now," he said as Collings grabbed for the gun.

"I need my gun." He reached across the table but stopped when Chris jammed the rifle into his ribs.

"Leave it."

"But..."

"I said leave it. Just get on your horse and ride." He gave Chris a go-to-Hades look and backed out the door. "You already kilt one man, aint' that enough? I ain't for letting you shoot-up no honest working posse. Them fellers got themselves families back home."

Chris kept pointing the rifle until he got mounted.

"You ain't giving me a fair chance, Mister. I can't very well defend myself without a gun," he said, turning the pony in a small circle.

"That's the life of an outlaw, sonny. Ain't much fun, is it? Better hurry. They ain't but a couple of miles behind me."

"Much obliged, Ma'am." He touched the brim of his hat and nodded toward Mrs. Shafer before galloping away. He hadn't quite disappeared over the next rise when the posse came into view. William ran toward them, yelling and waving. Sheriff Cunningham stopped long enough to hear what the boy was saying, before spurring his horse into a run with the others following. Chris watched until they were out of sight, then turned to shake a finger in front of Mrs. Shafer's nose.

"What do you mean running off like that and coming way out here by yourself?" Her eyes grew wide and filled with water as she stumbled backward inside the house.

"Ya not only put yourself in danger, but your children also. Didn't you even think of them? What's the matter with you, anyway?"

"Yes, I was thinking of them, Mr. Baker," she stammered.

"I doubt that, or you wouldn't have done it. And not only that, you stole my buggy and horses to boot." William eased his way inside the cabin and Chris handed him the rifle as he continued the scolding. She had backed across the room to cower against the opposite wall as he kept after her.

"And then, I come here to find a cut-throat sitting there and eating at your table? That feller don't need no gun. He cuts people into little pieces with his knife. How'd you like it if'n he'd kilt your children? Huh?"

She let out a wail as tears streamed from her eyes, and Chris felt everything inside of him melt. He threw his hands in the air and turned to grab the rifle from Billy. He started for the door, but stopped and threw his hat on the floor with a growl and stood staring at her. What he really wanted to do was take her in his arms and hug the dickens out of her, but that wouldn't do. He didn't know what to do with her. Paco was right. You couldn't leave a woman like that alone. She was set on getting herself into trouble no matter what. Chris knew she wasn't bad. She was just a head-strong Yankee set in her ways, and that's all there was to it. What was worse, he felt helpless around her.

"Oh, what's the use?" he said, grabbing his hat from the floor. "William? Let's you and me go take care of the animals."

"Yes, sir." He followed Chris out the door.

******

"Mr. Baker?"

"Ma'am?" He jumped up from where he had been seated on the porch for the past hour contemplating things. She had put the children to bed long ago and had been so quiet, Chris had taken it for granted she had gone to sleep herself.

"Isn't it rather cold here?"

"A might. But I had me some thinking to do, and I do it best at night, when things are quiet."

"Oh, I'm sorry. I must be disturbing your thinking."

"Not at all, Ma'am. Here, sit yerself," he said, and moved the empty apple crate toward her. "It concerns you anyway."

"What does? Your thinking?" she said, wrapping her shawl tight around her shoulders.

"Yes, Ma'am. I'm afraid I was a little harsh when I come busting through your door this evening. And, I would like to apologize for those things I said."

"No, you were quite within your boundaries for saying what you did. I had no idea that man was a murderer, and I did indeed steal your buggy and team. I am the one who should be apologizing to you. You just…frightened me with that gun. I thought you were going to kill Mr. Collings."

"Naw, I wouldn't have killed him. Well," he paused to shrug, "I might've, if he went ahead and pulled that hog-leg. But what I was afraid of was that posse, and him being holed-up inside this cabin with you and them younguns. No telling what might've happened. There would probably would have been some shooting and killing. You and them younguns might have been killed, or even worse. That's why I run him off the way I did, Ma'am. I just couldn't stand the thought of you or one of them getting hurt."

"That's awful nice of you, Mr. Baker," she said after a long silence. "I had no idea you felt that way about us. It's silly of me," she covered her face with the shawl and choked on the words, "I mean after the way you have treated us. Being so nice…spending money you can't afford, and looking out for our benefit." She looked at Chris with big watery eyes. "I'm sorry I'm such a pain."

"You ain't such a pain, Ma'am. I'm the one who's the pain. I shoulda taken you and them younguns and jumped aboard one of the riverboats and run that husband of yours down a week ago. Then, none of this would've happened."

"That's kind of you, Mr. Baker." She frowned with a nod. "But," she sighed, "I have a horrible feeling that my husband may have abandoned us for good. I don't think he wants us back, or he would have already been here."

"You don't really know that, Ma'am. He might have gotten himself hurt, or something terrible might have happened to hold him up. You can't just give up hoping."

"Oh, I haven't given up hope, Mr. Baker." She smiled and blinked back some tears. "But you know as well as I do that, barring death or sickness of some kind, he should have been back, or at the least, sent us word."

"Yes, Ma'am."

"That's why I insisted on coming back here. It's all the children and I have. And I'm afraid we won't be able to keep it much longer."

"Why's that, Ma'am?"

"Because, you were right, Mr. Baker. There is no water...not even for the single cow I have in the barn. A nice gentleman back at Hills Ferry explained that this house was constructed as a line-shack for sheepherders some years ago. The men who built it had to haul water from the creek a mile away when they stayed here. We had to do the same all summer long. I'm afraid we didn't have much of a vegetable garden. My husband and I were certainly foolish to buy it, thinking we could turn it into a real ranch. So," she heaved a sigh, "there is nothing left for me to do, except return home to my mother. And, I don't even have the means of doing that. I'm afraid, Mr. Baker, I don't know what to do."

Chris didn't have any idea what she would decide on doing, but he knew what he had to do, and it didn't include abandoning her and the kids. It meant finding her husband. Then, he could shuck things down to the cob and see what happened.

Chapter 11

He was up before daybreak and stoked a fire before heading toward the barn. There wasn't but a pitchfork or two of hay left, so Chris turned the animals loose to graze, before discovering there wasn't enough water left in any of the barrels for breakfast, let alone watering the animals. After hooking the walkers to the buggy and tossing every barrel and bucket he could find into the back seat, he set out for the creek, leading Bruiser and the cow behind. The sun had risen enough for him to see their smoke long before reaching the clump of oaks lining the bank. Chris readied the Winchester, then relaxed as he drew closer. It was Johnny Garcia and his family. There were fourteen of them, counting women and children, camping along the creek. Johnny gave Chris a broad grin and motioned him toward the fire where they were busy roasting a fresh-killed mule deer.

"My father wishes to thank you for the bear skin. It has brought him great luck."

"You can tell him he's welcome. I had no idea it would work that way, or I might've kept it, 'cause I ain't had nothing but rotten luck these past few weeks." Chris warmed his hands by the fire while the Indians communicated in their own language.

"My father says he still wishes to keep the skin, but he will say prayers for you."

"Much obliged," he said, with a nod toward the old man.

"Here, try some of the deer meat," Johnny said, holding the stick loaded with sizzling meat toward him. "It might help change your outlook on things this morning."

"Thanks." Chris sliced off a healthy portion, but found it too hot. He sat blowing on it while Johnny talked.

"You're staying at that old shack with that woman and her children, aren't you?"

"Yep. How'd you know that?" He bit off a hunk of meat and found it still too hot, and tried sucking in cold air, as a bunch of the younger children giggled.

"There's not much that happens around here that we don't know about. Where is that woman's husband?"

"Don't rightly know, but I aim to find out. Ain't right leaving her and them younguns stuck out there like that. The place ain't even got no water on it. That's what I'm doing down here right now."

"There's nothing wrong with the land, Chris. Not if you use it like it was meant to be used." Johnny sliced himself a hunk of meat and sat on his heels while studying him.

"And how's that?"

"Cattle and sheep. That's how that shack got there. My people built it for Alfas Basilo. He's the man who used to own the property. They stayed inside the cabin while they took care of his sheep and cattle. They watered the cattle and sheep right in this stream. It is good land, Chris. Only stupid people think they can make it something it isn't."

"Do the Shafers own this hunk of land too?"

"No. I understand they only bought the land the shack stands on."

"I wonder why?" Chris said, thoughtfully chewing a hunk of deer.

"Who knows?" Johnny said. "But you ought to buy this land, Chris, before someone else does."

"This right here with the creek?"

"Yes, it's for sale. And someone will buy it sooner or later. You could stay right there with the woman and build a herd of cattle or sheep, and water them right here."

"Well," Chris chuckled, "I might buy the land and build me a herd, but I can't stay there with Mrs. Shafer. She's a married woman, and I aim to find out about that husband of hers right soon."

"And then what? What will you do then? What if he doesn't want her? Or, maybe he's dead. What will you do then, Chris?"

Chris chewed his hunk of deer meat staring at him. *Danged smart-alec kid. Wonder where he got his learning from. Anyway, he's giving me a heap of thinking to do that I've been putting off long enough.*

"Wonder who owns this land with the creek?" he finally said, wiping his hands on his pant legs.

"I'm not sure, but I think Simon Newman does."

"Feller who owns the store in Hills Ferry?"

"Yes. I would ask him, if you're interested."

"I'm interested. You wouldn't know where a feller could buy him a few head of good cattle, would you?"

"Yes, I do." He grinned real big.

"Figures. I'll be gone a few days looking for that woman's husband. Make yourself available when I get back, and we'll talk business."

******

Mrs. Shafer and William looked fit to be tied when Chris brought the buggy to a halt in front of the cabin. The way she lit into him caused him to wonder if she didn't have a hornet caught inside her bonnet.

"What do you mean, frightening us like that? We thought you had taken the buggy and horses and abandoned us."

"Now, what would have given you that idea? I ain't left you yet, have I? William," he said to the boy, "give me a hand with these water buckets."

"Yes, you have," she said with her hands on her hips.

"I've what?"

"Abandoned us."

"I what?"

"Abandoned us. You…you ran off, doing God knows what, and left us alone in that wild, sinful town." She was crying and waving her arms in the air. "And then…then you show up, pointing a rifle at our dinner guest, calling him a murderer. And then I wake up this morning to find you and the buggy and animals gone…vanished. What was I to think, Mr. Baker?"

"The animals didn't have no water. I took them to the creek and hauled us back something to drink."

"You could have told me. Then, I wouldn't have worried so much," she yelled, before stomping back inside and slamming the door.

"Dad-blamed woman. How'd you get such a crazy woman for a mother, William?" He only grinned as he grabbed the bucket from Chris' hand.

"Anyone with a lick of sense should have known what I was up to. The animals needed caring for. Same as you folks," he said, hoisting a heavy barrel to the ground. "Bet she never even thought about the water. A crazy person like that wouldn't. They only think about things that pop into their little pea-brains. Now, she's got me acting crazy too. Here I am, standing in the back of this buggy, holding a bucket of water like a fool, arguing with a woman who don't make no sense."

"But, dag-nab-it," he said, staring at the door, "Johnny Garcia was right. What in the world am I going to do with y'all? Especially your mother."

William didn't say a word. He simply grinned, making Chris think the boy might had been struck with the same stupid-stick his mother had gotten whipped with.

Chapter 12

"Yes, I know who owns that land. I do," Simon said. He tossed a tin of tobacco several times thoughtfully. "Why do you ask?"

"Well, I've been doing me some powerful thinking, and I'd like to buy that hunk of land and raise me some cattle. That is, if you're willing to part with it."

"I don't know." He put the tobacco on the shelf and got down from the stepstool he'd been perched on. "I was considering growing some wheat on that piece myself. But I might be willing to part with it, if the price is right."

"And, what might that be?"

"There's three-hundred and twenty acres with a creek that runs almost year round. It only goes dry when there's a long period of no rain at all, and that isn't too often. And even then, you can usually find enough water for cattle or sheep by digging in the stream bed. Hmm, I'd say I'd be willing to let it go for ten dollars an acre, and that's a good price, mind you. I could probably get upwards of fifteen dollars, if I tried."

"I'll tell you what," Chris said, scribbling on a piece of paper, "I'll split the difference with you. I'll give you an even four thousand if you'll have someone drop off enough lumber and supplies on that flat berm above the creek to build a cabin. There's a family of Yokuts staying there. They'll be working for me when I get started." He handed Simon the note. "There's my pledge to give you the money when I get back in a week or so. One of them Yokuts, a young feller named Johnny Garcia, speaks better English than you and me put together. You can tell him what the lumber's for, and tell him to get started on the cabin. And, you might throw in a few things for his family too, if you don't mind."

"No, I don't mind," he hesitated, "but...are you sure you have that kind of money, Mr. Baker? I mean, four thousand dollars is a lot for a person like you to come up with."

"What kind of person am I, Mr. Newman?" Chris said, fishing a peppermint stick out of the jar for William.

"I don't know exactly. know you're kind and generous. Anyone can see that by the way you've taken care of Mrs. Shafer and her family. But, I took it for granted that you're just an average, hardworking man struggling to make a living like everyone else around here. Are you sure you have that much money?"

"Well, let me tell you something." he leaned across the counter. "I *am* a hardworking man struggling to make ends meet. And I reckon I'll be that way 'til the day I die. But, to answer your question, yes I know where I can get that much money, and I'll bring it to you in the form of a bank draft when I get back into town." He tossed a penny on the counter. "That's for the candy."

"Ah, may I ask where you're going, Mr. Baker?" Simon shouted as Chris reached the door.

"I reckon I'm going to do what I should have done in the first place. I'm taking Mrs. Shafer and her younguns down river on one of them steamers to see if we can find out what happened to her man."

******

They happened on Sheriff Cunningham and his posse early next morning while they were at the dock buying passage for San Francisco on the *Georgiana*. The Sheriff had Richard Collings, in handcuffs. He said they had caught him holed-up inside a coal mine on Mt. Diablo, and were preparing to take the ferry across the river. Chris explained what his own plans were, and asked Sheriff Cunningham if he happened to hear anything about Mrs. Shafer's husband to let Simon Newman know, since he planned on checking in with him on a regular basis.

"I'm sorry, Ma'am," Sheriff Cunningham said as he removed his hat. "I don't know anything about your husband. "This gentleman," he nudged Collings, "has kept me kinda busy. But I'll do some checking around just as soon as I get back to my office."

"Thank you, sir," Mrs. Shafer said with a little curtsy, and stood watching until they had completely crossed the river.

Passage downriver for the four of them on the paddle-wheeler cost a dollar, excluding meals. Chris argued that it should've been only seventy-five cents, seeing as Edith was brand new and wouldn't take up much room. The grizzled old man behind the ticket counter said they were getting a deal with two separate rooms with beds for the price, and that he shouldn't be complaining.

"Especially, seeing as how the same thing cost thirty dollars a head a few years ago."

"I don't care what things *used* to cost. I only care what I've gotta pay in the right here and now." Chris gave the dollar, but called him a bandit for good measure.

He stored their grip inside the rooms and William ran out to nose around on the deck. Chris yelled for him to stay where they could keep an eye on him, then waited by the railing while Mrs. Shafer shut herself inside to feed Edith. Her room was next to his with a connecting door, much like the hotel, except the rooms were smaller. The captain pulled away from the dock with several long blasts of the steam whistle. Black clouds of smoke poured from the stacks as the paddlewheel churned against the current. He laughed as William, acting as though he had won the world, darted up and down the deck shouting and waving to the folks on shore. Mrs. Shafer had Edith all rolled up like a papoose when she joined them on deck.

"She asleep?"

"Mmhum," she said with a smile. "Her tummy is full and she's all warm and cozy."

"Speaking of tummies, mine's beginning to think my throat's been cut. What do you say about us going to see what kind of vittles they've got aboard this here tub?"

"That would be nice. I am rather hungry myself."

He took her by the arm and led her toward the galley. It took some convincing to get William to go peaceably. Chris had to promise he could spend the majority of the trip on deck, which meant he had to be with him. Chris was about a second away from tanning William's hide by the time they got seated, and was hoping Mr. Shafer himself would be the one waiting on their table. Then, he could simply turn his little boy over to him. But their steward, who happened to be nice enough, turned out to be a short, fat Mexican with a faceful of black stubble.

Although the food was more than tolerable tasting, Chris couldn't find much that resembled anything he was used to eating. Mrs. Shafer laughed at the way he balked when they shoved a plateful of eggs topped with melted cheese in front of him. He promptly told her if he'd wanted cheese, he would've asked for cheese. But seeing as how he had asked for eggs, he half expected to get a plate of eggs. And instead of having a bowl of fruit on the side, he was used to getting a bowl of red beans or grits for breakfast.

When they had finished eating, they took a leisurely stroll on the deck from one end to the other, looking things over. Chris held the baby as Mary Shafer tucked her hand inside his arm and talked excitedly about the scenery they were passing. Chris admitted it was as pretty a site as one could hope to see. Besides the endless landscape filled with oaks, cottonwoods and brush, he counted close to thirty deer and elk darting up the banks as they passed. Once they even spied a mother bear with her cub hiding in the brush and watching. The captain gave a long blast on the whistle, and sent the mother and her cub bounding through the trees.

He left Mrs. Shafer at her door shortly after midday, and had to fight with William to get him to take his afternoon nap. He argued he was too old to be taking naps. Chris couldn't put up much of an argument there, seeing as he had been plowing fields by the time he was six or seven. It was Mrs. Shafer herself that put a stop to his whining when she stuck her head through the connecting door and said she was going to tan his backside if he didn't shut his mouth and get in the bed. The boy crawled into bed, but not without one final whine.

"I'm warning you," she said waving a finger in the air. Chris had to admit, she knew her son a whole lot better than he did. William had not closed his eyes more than a minute before he was fast asleep.

Chris wasn't sleepy by a long shot, so he eased himself out the door and wandered around the deck asking folks if they'd seen anyone matching George Shafer's description. Everyone he asked said they couldn't recall anyone by that name or description, although the ship's first mate said he remembered someone like that hanging around the docks in Stockton. Chris thanked him, and found a spot near a young boy who was fishing off the side of the boat. It didn't look like he was having any more luck than Chris was. But, he knew his luck had better change right quick, or he would be in sad shape. Holding Edith in his arms with Mrs. Shafer's hand tucked inside his elbow had felt too comfortable not to be dangerous. And the thought of handing them over to a man that had abandoned them gave Chris a great big empty spot in the middle of his chest. *Nope*, he thought to himself. *I'm gonna have to find George Shafer and do it right soon, or I might not be willing to hand his family over*. And Chris had never took much to anyone who went around stealing other men's wives. He kind of thought of them as being worse than an honest cow thief or bank robber. He'd met up with a couple of rustlers and at least one bank robber after the war, and they were simply fellows who'd lost everything to Yankee carpetbaggers and were trying to survive. But how could you trust a man that would steal another man's family? He no more got that reminder into his pea-brain, when he started thinking how he wouldn't really be stealing her, seeing as George Shafer had been the one who'd run off and left them out at Poverty Flat in the first place.

"Aw, Christian Michael Baker, you're dumber than a rotten post," he said out loud.

"What was that, mister?" The boy holding the cane pole looked up at him.

"Nothing. Just talking to myself," he said, shoving his hands deep into his pockets with a shrug. He had to find that woman's husband right soon, or become a babbling idiot. But how? Finding one man he had never met in a city the size of Stockton or San Francisco would be like finding a live rabbit inside a den of hungry foxes. But, no one even knew if George Shafer was in either place. He might not even be in California. For all they knew, he could've sprouted wings and flown to the moon.

He turned back toward the cabin feeling lower than a lizard's belly.

Chapter 13

Chris stared at the darkened ceiling, wishing there was some way for a fellow to know what was in a woman's mind. Then, maybe he could bottle it inside a Mason jar, or write it in a book for other men to read. But he had never known anyone who could figure what a female-critter was thinking, so no books or jars of such knowledge existed. And he would be hanged if he could understand what he had done to upset her on their last evening in San Francisco.

They had not been able to find Mrs. Shafer's husband in in any of the places they stopped. Trying to find one person in a city the size of San Francisco had been impossible. Chris had tried making the experience pleasant by turning it into a sightseeing excursion, but he knew the trip was starting to wear on Mrs. Shafer something fierce. Chris' brother, James, had always claimed Chris had a talent for sticking his foot in his mouth, even when he was trying to be nice, and Chris had to reckon that was so. But he still couldn't decide what he had said or done that evening that would offend her. He had been, in his opinion, the perfect gentleman. He had even let her pick where they were going to take in vittles.

He almost died when she chose a French restaurant. It was a nice enough looking place, but he couldn't read a thing on the menu, and he wouldn't have fed one of his ma's hogs some of the things he saw on people's plates. The man seated at the table next to theirs had a plate full of snails. But there he sat, staring, and moving the funny-looking stuff she had ordered round his plate with a fork, trying to make pleasant conversation, when he must have jammed both boots into his mouth at once. And trying his best, he still couldn't decide what started the whole thing, but Chris had a suspicion it was that stuff on his plate. If they had eaten at any normal place, he would have been shoveling grub down his gullet like a hungry wolf, instead of wondering what was on his plate. Then, he heard her mention how she should take her children and head back east to live with her parents.

"Reckon I wouldn't like that none."

"And why's that, Mr. Baker?"

"Ma'am?" He glanced at her seated across the table, then back to the funny looking things on his plate.

"I was saying that I think I should swallow my pride and write my parents, asking for passage home, and perhaps some money to repay you for your kindness. And you said you wouldn't like for me to do that. I simply asked why you should feel that way. I know we have been a huge bother and expense to you."

"No, you haven't been much of a bother, and don't worry about the money. I've got me a little saved, and I might as well spend it on you and these younguns as on some foolishness for myself. Well, maybe a little. I mean about the bother...not the money," he added with a grin. "I know I complain and grumble once in awhile, but you ain't much of a bother a'tall. None of you." He glanced around the table, then took a second look at William. He had the same things on his plate that Chris had on his, but the way the boy was shoveling it down caused him to wonder if there wasn't something wrong with him.

"Well, we can't live off your generosity forever, Mr. Baker. It has been embarrassing enough as it is. And you can't deny that I've caused you to be angry on several occasions."

"No, Ma'am, I don't deny that. But, there's other things to consider," he said.

"Like what?"

Chris laid his fork in his plate and took his time sipping coffee from the midget-sized cup they had set the table with, hoping she'd change the conversation and talk about something else.

"Mr. Baker, I'm waiting," she said with a smile.

"Ma'am?"

"You said there were other things for me to consider before leaving California. I'm waiting for you to tell me what they are."

"Well, for one, that place of yours. I know Poverty Flat ain't much right now, but it can be."

"Excuse me," she giggled, "what did you call our farm?"

"Poverty Flat. That's what you called it that day we all headed into town to attend Sunday meeting. Remember?"

"No, I don't. But it does fit, doesn't it? You may continue calling it *Poverty Flat* if you wish." She reached across the table and squeezed his arm, before turning to check on Edith. She had the baby rolled in a blanket and stuck inside a wicker basket, reminding Chris of that day's baked goods. But Edith didn't seem to mind being stuck inside a basket, and had been fast asleep before they were seated at the table. Mrs. Shafer glanced up and smiled warmly.

"I distinctly remember your telling me on several occasions that our farm was a hopeless cause, and you argued with me something fierce every time I wanted to return. Why the change of heart, Mr. Baker? I thought you would be happy to see us leave that place."

"Yes, Ma'am. But most of my talk was just out of my bad side, because I didn't like seeing y'all stuck out there like you was. It wasn't safe. And I ain't changed my mind none about y'all living like a pack of rats. But I've been talking to Johnny Garcia, he's an Injun friend of mine, and he says that place of your'n can be turned into something downright pleasant. He says y'all have just been trying to make it into something it wasn't meant to be. In fact, he claims that little cabin was built as a line shack for sheepherders, and they used to haul water up there when it was in use."

"I am quite aware of that, Mr. Baker. Remember my saying so?"

"Yes, Ma'am, I reckon I do."

She propped her elbows on the table and allowed her chin to rest against her knuckles as she studied him. "And what, in your opinion, should I do with our farm?"

"Well, raise cattle, for one thing. It's some of the finest grazing land I've seen anywhere."

"Yes, I'll agree with you. You might not know this about me, Mr. Baker, but I do know a little about cattle. I grew up on a farm."

"No, Ma'am, I didn't."

"It's true. My parents have a very successful place of their own in New York state. They happen to raise some of the finest cattle in the world. But," she paused to take a sip of coffee and grin, "seeing as *Poverty Flat*, as you have chosen to name it, has no water, and seeing as I have no money to buy cattle…how do you propose I do such a thing?"

"Well, water ain't no problem, Ma'am. I haven't had the chance to tell you yet, but I'm buying the place right next to yours, with a creek that runs most year-round. That's why I insisted on going to the bank today. And as far as cattle are concerned. I'm fixing to buy a few head myself. I could lend you some until you build up a herd of your own."

"How convenient. I had no idea you were considering the land next to ours. And your offer is more than generous," she said. Chris sat wondering what was inside her head as she took her time checking on Edith, who had let out a whimper. "But," she glanced up, "how are we supposed to survive without food and water until that happens?"

"Well, I've done got the water problem figured out. We'll get us a water wagon and haul water from the creek on my place up to yours. I've seen it done before. In the meantime, we might even be able to sink a well somewhere near your house. I'm thinking about having one sunk on my place, just so's I can have water during the dry seasons."

"I see." She grew somber and stared at her plate for a minute. "You have been doing quite a bit of *figuring*, haven't you? But I'm afraid that it is impossible."

"Begging you pardon, Ma'am, but it's quite possible. I've spent my whole life working cattle, except for when I was in the war, and I know them critters like the back of my hand. And I've seen things like this done."

"Yes, I am certain your plans for us and our land are quite sound. But, there is something you have forgotten, Mr. Baker."

"What's that, Ma'am?"

"I would have to agree to something like that, wouldn't I?"

"Yes, Ma'am. But…"

"I think I had better return to my room. Edith needs feeding," she said, as a tear spilled over to run down one cheek. "I'll wait for you inside the carriage." She scooted away from the table and grabbed the baby. Chris watched her walk ramrod straight out the door before turning toward William.

"What'd I say?"

"Heck if I know." Chris decided there *was* something wrong with the boy. He not only cleaned his own plate, but took a spoonful of the funny looking things off Chris's before leaving.

Chapter 14

There wasn't but maybe a dozen folks that Chris had run into over the years that he could say he honestly disliked, but, Frank Sorenson was at the top of the of the list, and he was a southerner to boot. They had no more than got off the *Georgiana* before running smack into him and that partner of his, Billy. The men were leaning against the railing in front of *The Nugget*, that one being the closest saloon to the river. Both men were already drunk, and it was only two hours past noon.

"That's why he didn't want to go to Columbia with us Bill," Frank said, as Chris held onto Mrs. Shafer's arm and tried weaving their way past them. "He's been too busy stealing another man's wife to be bothered with helping us win the war."

Chris stiffened, but kept walking.

"That right, Nails? You'd rather steal another man's wife, than help us out?" Billy said, laughing. "She must be pretty good, if that's the case," he continued as they followed them down the street. "Of course, you can't blame him none. I'd kinda like some of her company myself." People on the sidewalks, sensing trouble, began seeking the shelter of doorways.

"That right, Nails? Is she that good?" Frank said, and grabbed Chris' arm.

Before he thought, he had backhanded Frank across the mouth, landing him on his backside at Billy's feet, where he scrambled halfway to his feet and grabbed for his gun. Chris let go of Mrs. Shafer's arm and kicked him real hard in the gut and he folded over with a groan. Chris tossed the gun across the street and poked a finger in Billy's face.

"Don't even think about slapping leather with me, boy. It ain't worth dying for."

"Na-uh, Nails," he said, lifting both hands away from his body. "I ain't nearly as stupid as my pard, here."

Chris took Mrs. Shafer by the arm and hurried her and William toward the hotel. Neither of them said a word until he had seen them inside her room.

"You weren't going to kill that man because of me, were you, Mr. Baker?" Her eyes were big and dark against her pale cheeks.

"No, not unless he pulled that iron of his. Then, I guess I'd have had to kill him, or get myself kilt. Why?"

"I just didn't want to see anyone hurt or killed over some small, meaningless incident like that," she said, and turned away.

"Begging your pardon, Ma'am, but that weren't no small incident. That feller was insinuating things and trying to sully your honor."

"I know that, Mr. Baker. I was there." She turned to glare at him. "But there are some things that are worth dying for, and that certainly wasn't one of them."

"Well, I'll grant that you're right on that one. And just in case you didn't notice, I tried walking away, but them fellers wouldn't let me. And I could've pulled my iron and kilt them both deader'n Solomon, but I didn't, because neither of them boys needed killing. They needed a beating, and, that's just what I would've done, except I had you and the boy with me."

"And that is supposed to make me feel better, is it?"

"I reckon."

"Well, it doesn't," she yelled in his face. "This...this whole thing makes me sick." She waved her arms in the air. "The fact that my husband abandoned us in that shack without food and water - And the fact that everyone thinks we are somehow lovers - And now you are being forced into fighting and perhaps killing someone because of my honor. I know you are kind, and generous and only trying to help. But...don't you see how this has turned out?" She covered her face with her hands and cried. "Oh, leave me alone. Just get out! Go away and leave me alone."

He glanced at William and the boy shrugged as if to say, "heck if I know," so Chris did as she said. He stomped all the way to Reb's livery to see how Bruiser and the animals were doing. Bruiser acted mighty happy to see him. And Mrs. Shafer's cow had packed some weight onto her ribs the few days they were gone. Chris told Reb to have them all, including the buggy, ready to travel the next morning, since he planned to take Mrs. Shafer back to her place. Reb said that was fine, but was going to miss the cow, seeing as she had been giving enough milk for him and his neighbor's families every morning.

Next, Chris went to the general store to give Simon Newman the bank draft he'd gotten in San Francisco, and signed the papers.

"You're now the owner of one of the finest spreads in the San Joaquin Valley, and a lucky man," Simon said, shaking Chris' hand. "I came close to changing my mind while you were gone, but, I'm a man of my word, and a deal is a deal."

"I'm glad you didn't."

"Anyway, I took you at you word and delivered more than enough building materials to the site you spoke of, along with plenty of dry goods. Are you sure those Indians know how to build your cabin? They started moving things around even before I left."

"I didn't expect them to do the building, and I don't rightly know if they know how. Reckon we'll find out, won't we?"

"I guess so. You just might have the fanciest hogan anywhere, considering the amount of planking and nails I delivered."

"Maybe, but that might not be so bad." Chris started to leave when he spied the small bore rifle hanging behind the counter.

"That new?"

"No, it actually belonged to a miner who was down on his luck. He traded it for a sack of beans, a couple pounds of bacon and a few dollars." Simon took the gun off the rack and handed it across the counter. "Took real good care of it, though. Looks brand new."

"Can't be but a couple of years old as it is," Chris said, giving the gun the once-over. "Rolling block Remington. .32 caliber with a pistol grip and walnut stock. Must've been special ordered. I ain't seen but one like it. What are you asking for it?"

"How about forty dollars, and I'll throw in a couple of boxes of shells."

"It's a deal," he said, digging into his pocket.

"Kind of a small gun for a big man like you, isn't it?" he said, pulling the boxes of shells from under the counter. "I thought you'd be more into a heavier type of arm."

"You thought right." Chris laid the money on the counter. "I'm sorta partial to my forty-four-forty. I just got me a hunch it might become kinda handy."

******

He watched as Mrs. Shafer mailed her letter to her parents asking for help, then took them down the street to buy everyone a meal he could actually eat. It was over a plateful of steak, beans, fried taters, hot buttered biscuits and a pot of hot coffee that he told her she'd better pack her grip.

"And why's that, Mr. Baker?"

"Because I'm taking y'all back out to your place first thing in the morning."

"Really? And why, may I ask, would I want to return to a place that holds nothing for me? You've even taken my

Poverty Flat

cow and horse and placed them in that stable with the funny little man at the end of town."

Chris paused with a forkful of beans to stare at her. He reckoned to be a little slow sometimes, especially when it came to womenfolk. He could never figure out his sister for instance, and how quickly she could change her mind about things. But the woman seated across the table from him was the most confoundedness one he had ever met. He laid the knife and fork down and continued staring.

"Now, that don't make no sense at all, Ma'am."

"What doesn't?"

"Your not wanting to go back to your own place. One minute I'm almost having to use blasting powder to get you outta there, and the next, I can't seem to get ya talked into going back out there. You're enough to make a preacher cuss."

"That's a woman's right to change her mind anytime she wants to." She smiled. "And, might I remind you Mr. Baker, that without my husband, there is really no reason for my being there."

"Now, that just ain't so, Ma'am," he said shaking his head. "You got yourself a real nice spread out there. Granted, it's gonna take a little work fixing it up, but it can be turned into something to really be proud of."

"Thank you. That is a very kind thing to say. But, the only reason I insisted on being there in the first place was that it seemed to give me some hope that my husband might return, and things would be alright again. But now, there doesn't seem to be any hope of that ever happening, does it? So, there is no reason for my being there."

"I hate to disagree with you, Ma'am, but there's every reason for your being there."

"Really?" She crinkled her eyebrows and folded her hands in front of her. "Give me one."

"Okay, the boy. He's got to have a place of his own to plant his roots. And what about Edith. Sure, she's too small to care about much right now. But come real soon, she's gonna want to call some place home."

"They can have that at my parent's farm. Besides, I don't plan on living with my parents forever. I *do* plan on renting a place of my own someday. It might take awhile...maybe after I'm able to find employment and get back on my feet. But it will happen," she said with nod of finality.

"I reckon. But you can't outrun the fact that you was abandoned and hurt, no matter the miles you're able to put between yourself and *Poverty Flat*."

Her chin quivered as she stared at her plate. "That was a horrible thing to say."

"Granted, but it needed saying. Now, I don't rightly care none if you pack up your kids and go back home to mama. That's your business, and I ain't got no say-so in the matter. But I'm recommending that in the meantime, you go back out there to have at least a look-see and settle things in you mind, to see if this leaving's what you really want."

"Okay, Mr. Baker," she said with a sniff. "you're right. I'll go with you whenever you say. Just to have a *look-see* as you called it. I'm not promising I'll change my mind and stay, mind you."

"I never thought you would," he said, and winked at William. The boy grinned and kept shoveling the food like he hadn't eaten in a hundred years.

******

They left at daybreak and had breakfast in Dutch Corners, then went on to Poverty Flat, taking only the buggy. Chris had decided it was a safer bet to leave the cow and two other horses behind, not knowing which way her mind might swing. Things hadn't changed much, except the place looked clean and slept in. By the small pile of corn inside a stone grinding bowl he figured some of the Yokuts had been using her cabin to sleep in, and stated as much. Mrs. Shafer simply raised her eyebrows and smiled.

"They have certainly kept it clean. There's even water in the barrels on the porch."

They climbed back in the buggy and headed to where they were working on the cabin, and Chris stopped on the rise above the creek to stare. The cabin was nearly built, except it wasn't exactly what one would call a cabin. It looked more like a full-blown house, with a porch running completely around the outside and glass windows. One of the younger Indian boys was busy whitewashing the outside as they parked in front.

"Hello there!" Johnny Garcia yelled from where he was busy nailing shingles on the roof peak. "We were wondering when you would get back. I have a few questions for you." He slid down the roof toward a homemade ladder while a couple more Indians continued pounding away on the shingles.

"Yeah," Chris said, helping Mrs. Shafer from the buggy. "And I have a few questions for you, too. When, and how, did y'all do all this?"

"Simon delivered the lumber a couple of days after you left, and we got started. You didn't tell us what you wanted. So," he shrugged "I hope it's alright."

"Alright?" Chris said, letting his eyes wander as he walked around the house. He paused as he spied the huge stack of lumber Simon Newman had delivered at the rear of the house.

"Seems to me you used mighty little building this here house. You got some sort of gift, kinda like Jesus, when he fed five thousand folks with a couple of catfish and five biscuits?"

"No," Johnny said with a laugh. "Actually, I knew of this house long before you decided to buy this property. A homesteader a few miles south of here had it almost completed when he got gored by a bull and died. He was married to a very young girl, who decided she'd rather live in San Francisco than on their homestead. I bought the complete house, in your name of course, for two hundred dollars. We borrowed several flatbed wagons and mules, then took it apart, wall by wall, and moved it here."

"I had no idea y'all knew how to do such a thing. I figured I'd have to hire someone from town, or throw something together myself. This is more than I expected. This is great! Where did you learn such a thing?"

"My brother and I learned about tools in the Mission school. Then we both worked for a German carpenter in Grayson, building houses. So, we just copied what we learned from him. Come inside and let me show you what we've done."

Chris waited a couple more minutes before entering the house, where he found Johnny showing Mrs. Shafer the cupboards and sink board inside the kitchen, with a walk-in pantry. She took her time running her fingers over the smooth pine doors as she eyed the cupboards, and Chris began realizing how natural such a thing must be for a woman. It was then she asked the question he should have asked outside.

"Mr. Baker, shouldn't you be asking Mr. Garcia where he got the two hundred dollars to buy this house?"

"I borrowed it," Johnny said. "In his name, of course. He's the one in debt, not me."

Johnny continued the tour with the bedrooms, where he bragged about the storage space in the window seats and wardrobes. The place had three bedrooms, and Chris said it was a terrible waste of lumber. He only had need of one, and they could have used the rest of the lumber for something else. That was, unless he figured on moving in the house himself.

"No, I plan on using the lumber you bought from Simon to build a bunk house over near the proposed corral, with your permission, of course. Right in the middle of that clump of oak trees," he said pointing to a spot downstream. "But we'll need more lumber before we can complete the corral. That is, unless we are all fired. In that case, we'll just pack up and fade back into the hills like good Indians." He finished with a huge grin, and a wink at Mrs. Shafer.

"No, you ain't fired. None of you are. I'm impressed with what you've done. And that's the perfect spot for a bunkhouse and corral. You seem to know as much about ranching as I do. But I still can't figure on the extra bedrooms. I can't be using them, unless I got myself a passel of company."

Johnny stared at Chris before glancing toward Mrs. Shafer and back again. "I don't know. I just thought you might have plans of your own and be needing them some day."

Chris didn't say anything, but Mrs. Shafer's face turned red as she pretended to check on Edith. Johnny led the way outside, where he introduced his family. There were a few who spoke English, some better than others, but Chris caught on quickly that a few didn't understand a lick of what he was saying. He found them friendly, and they prepared a midday meal of roasted venison with corn bread that resembled a thick tortilla. They washed it down with ice cold water from the creek, and sat in the shade of the porch, chatting. Johnny's twelve-year-old sister, Cola`we, took a liking to Mrs. Shafer, and followed her around most of the afternoon. Chris asked if the girl's name had any special meaning, and Johnny said the English translation would be *Lily*.

"Well," Chris said, watching the girl laugh at something Mrs. Shafer had said. "That's a right pretty name for a mighty pretty girl."

Some of the Indian boys wanted to take William sightseeing, and Chris asked them to wait. He went to the buggy and returned with the new rifle.

"Any of you fellers know how to use one of these things?" He held the Remington high for them to see.

"Miguel does." Johnny motioned to one of the older boys. "He handles a gun better than I do."

"Here," he said, tossing him the gun. "You'll find a box of shells in the luggage compartment of the carriage. "Teach William here how to use it. But I don't want nothing kilt but cactus or tree stumps."

"No ,William." Mrs. Shafer stood up as the boys started to leave. "I don't want you playing with guns."

"Begging your pardon, Ma'am, but the boy ain't gonna be playing. He's gonna be learning. Go on boy," he said to William. "Let's see if you can't learn to shoot some."

"Mr. Baker," she said indignantly, "who do you think you are? You should have asked me before saying such a thing. That is the most ridiculous thing I have seen you do yet. Guns are dangerous, and I would rather my son doesn't learn how to handle one."

"Well, now," he grinned, "that's mighty high talk coming from a woman who introduced herself with a shotgun."

"That was different. I was frightened."

"Yes, and it was the proper thing to do, because it scared the dickens out of me. Look," he said, taking her by the shoulders, "a gun is no different than any other tool. It was in the back of that buggy all the way here and never hurt a soul. I'll guarantee that some of the people who use guns are dangerous, but you can kill a man just as easy with Johnny's hammer as you can with that rifle."

"Yes, but I don't see any need of my son learning to handle one. I don't want him thinking of that gun as a way of stopping arguments, like that drunken man back in Hills Ferry."

"I don't think you need to be worrying about William that way none. He's got you to teach him right from wrong. And I'll be around to help him some myself, for that matter. That is, until you go back east to your mama."

They paused at the crack of the rifle, and walked to the edge of the porch to watch the boys taking pop-shots at a tree stump. Mrs. Shafer grimaced at the sound of another shot. It was her son holding the rifle.

"He's a mighty fine boy, Mrs. Shafer. Let him grow up to be a fine man." He left her on the porch to help Johnny tote a couple of bundles of shingles up the ladder. He paused at the base of the ladder to look at her.

"Don't forget where you are, Ma'am. You might be needing him to know how to shoot that rifle before you leave."

Chapter 15

It was dark when they arrived in Hills Ferry. After a quick meal in the hotel of hot soup and freshly baked bread, he saw Mrs. Shafer and Edith to their room. William was as talkative as any boy his age, but Chris decided he must have been exhausted, because he was asleep within a minute after being tucked into bed. That left Chris with time and a lot of powerful thinking to do. He laid awake most of the night trying to get it done, and the conclusion he came to was one he hadn't wanted to face.

After shucking right to the cob, the fact was, he didn't really want Mrs. Shafer taking the kids back to New York. He had grown mighty fond of each and every one of them, including her. Besides, if she raised them at her folk's place, that would turn them into Yankees, when there wasn't any need of that happening. On the other hand, there wasn't any way of him stopping her from going. Not without finding her husband, and it didn't look like that was going to happen. Besides, even if he did find him, and could talk some sense into the man, that would mean she would be married to his neighbor and they would be living like a bunch of rats on Poverty Flat.

On the other hand, if Chris couldn't find him, which was likely the case, he still couldn't make her stay. Without a husband, dead or alive, there wasn't anything tying her to that hunk of land. The sun was beginning to peek through the window when he decided it was best just to let her do what she wanted…which was more than likely what she would do, regardless of what he had to say.

"Ma'am," he said over a plateful of eggs, "I think you should go back home to your folks' place back east."

"Oh, and why is that, Mr. Baker?"

"Well, I hate to say it, but it ain't likely that we're gonna find you husband. At least, not alive anyways. Something's had to have happened that's been keeping him away this long."

"I know that," she said, lowering her head like she was praying. "We both do…William and I."

Chris looked at the boy, who's eyes darted back and forth between the two adults, before landing on his plate.

"I'm really sorry to be the one having to say it."

"No, Mr. Baker, you're right." She smiled and sniffed. "I guess I've known it all along. My husband is gone. That is why I was willing to write my parents, asking for their help." She rummaged around inside the bag for a handkerchief and blew her nose. "Excuse me," she said with a weak smile. "William and I both understand."

"Yes, Ma'am. In the meantime, reckon you and the boy might be able to stay here in town by yourselves a few days while I take care of some things out at my place?"

"I am certain we will be fine, Mr. Baker. You have been more than kind, so don't worry about us. In fact," she paused to stuff the hanky back inside the bag, "I've been thinking that I might try to find something to do…some part-time employment, while I am waiting. It will take some weeks for my letter to arrive, and then I'll have to wait for the reply. There's simply no reason for me to be sitting around and waiting, is there?"

"No, Ma'am. The work will probably do you some good. Got any idee what you might be doing?"

"No, but I'm certain that in a busy town such as this, there must be something. I am decently educated."

"Just so you don't go getting the idea of working in one of them saloons as a dance hall girl."

"No, Mr. Baker," she laughed, "I will certainly not consider working as a dance hall girl. In fact, I will probably ask Reverend Gibson's wife for some advice. I'm sure she will know of something I can do."

"Yes, Ma'am. I'm sure."

******

Early the next morning Chris took Bruiser and a wagonload of tools and building supplies to where Johnny Garcia and his family were building the house. They had almost finished the place and, in Chris' opinion, it was looking down right pretty, almost too good for the likes of him. He put most of the boys to building the bunkhouse and corral while he and Johnny finished nailing the last boards onto the house. He found the Indians to be friendly, fun-loving folk, and was having a right good time. Then, about three days after Chris had arrived, Reb came riding up with the boy.

"Hate to bother you, Captain. But this here boy's pa arrived in town, and all hell's broke loose." Reb took a seat on the shaded porch as Johnny's ma poured him a hot cup of coffee.

"Do tell. Then why ain't William back there swapping howdies with his pa, instead of traipsing all the way out here with the likes of you?"

"Better ask him that."

"William?" Chis said, and had to wait a long minute while the boy shuffled his feet back and forth.

"Well, Pa's holed up inside the saloon and won't come out to talk to Mom."

"And what's she doing?"

"She's standing out in the street calling for him to come out." He shrugged and stared at his feet.

"That's right, Captain. One hell of a sight. Must be close to a hundred people all standing around and talking. Some of them's laughing and calling her a crazy woman. That preacher's wife's been trying to get her to leave, but she won't budge. Well, you know how stubborn she is."

"I reckon," he said, and removed the nail apron.

"Johnny, you think you can handle things while I'm gone?"

"You bet'cha, boss."

"Yeah, I suppose you can," Chris said with a chuckle. He figured the Indian could handle most anything that came along without his help, and also reckoned that he had better do whatever it took to see that Johnny and his folks stayed right there, working for him. Not that he didn't know anything about cattle, because that was all Chris had done, except for the time spent fighting in the war. But having someone who knew what they were doing without having to be told was more valuable than having a pot of gold, anyway you looked at it.

It didn't take long to saddle Bruiser and head toward Hills Ferry. Chris found himself having to hold the huge animal in check, since the roan Reb was riding and the pony William had were tired from the trip out to the ranch. They arrived an hour before sundown and, just as Reb had told him, there stood Mrs. Shafer, like a blooming idiot, calling for her no-account husband to come out and talk to her.

"Ma'am," Chris said, taking her by the arm, "may I ask what you're doing?"

"Trying to get my husband to talk to me." She was sunburned and had a raspy voice.

"And you've been out here most of the day?"

"Yes, Mr. Baker, I have."

"Ma'am, I reckon your husband doesn't want to, or he'd already have been here."

"I know, Mr. Baker. But he *is* my husband. And he needs to at least see his daughter, and let us know what his plans are."

"I reckon I can tell you what his plans are, Ma'am." Chris was fighting hard to keep his temper in check, but was afraid it was a losing battle.

"So can I, Mr. Baker. But he still needs to see his daughter and tell me in person."

"Yes, Ma'am." He glanced around at the grinning crowd that had gathered to laugh at someone who was in obvious pain.

"Where's Edith?"

"She's with Pastor Gibson's wife," she said, as tears began to spill over.

"You wait right here, Ma'am," he said, and handed her his neckerchief. "I'll go fetch your man for you."

Chris pushed his way inside and waited a minute for his eyes to adjust to the dimness of the room. "Which one of you yahoos is George Shafer?"

"Right here, if it's any of your concern," said a short, stocky man seated at a poker game.

"Your wife's waiting outside to talk to you."

"So I heard. You the man that's been sporting her around while I've been gone?"

"Depends on what you consider *sporting*." Chris moved closer to where he was sitting. "I saw they had a roof over their heads, and something to eat, seeing as you weren't around to take care of them."

"I'll bet that isn't all." He looked up and sniggered. "And what did you get in return?"

He had no more than gotten the words out, when Chris kicked the chair from under him. He came up cussing and charged like a bull with it's head down. Chris was used to wrestling with his brothers and the boys he had grown up with, so he simply sidestepped the raging man, and caught him by the collar and the back of the britches as he passed, then politely toss him through the doors and onto the street.

He crawled to his feet calling Chris names he couldn't repeat in mixed company, and grabbed for his gun. Chris pounced on him before he could clear leather, and smashed him with a hard right that spun him around and to his knees. He grabbed the gun from Shafer's holster and tossed it toward William, who let it fall in the dust. Shafer shook off the blow and charged again, swinging haymakers that caught nothing but air. Chris circled, waiting for his turn. Shafer paused to catch his breath, and Chris snapped a couple of lefts into his nose, followed by a short right that caused him to wobble.

He stepped back, thinking the fight was over, but Shafer caught him glancing at Mrs. Shafer and swung a vicious right that knocked Chris back into the crowd. He landed on his backside just as Shafer landed on top, kicking, biting and scratching like a woman. Chris bellowed like a angry bull and kicked Shafer away as he came up swinging both fists. He was on top of him, and pounding away, when he heard Mrs. Shafer's voice behind him, "Mr. Baker! Will you please quit beating my husband?"

He backed away and took a look, and the man lying in the street was a bloody mess. Chris drug him by the collar, and shoved the top half of him into the watering trough. Then hauled him to where Mrs. Shafer stood with William.

"Here he is, Ma'am. Sorry about the little ruckus. But it took some doing to get him to face the music."

******

Chris was hitched up to Reverend Gibson's table eating apple pie and drinking coffee when Mrs. Shafer knocked on the door. She seated herself across the table and quietly accepted a cup for herself. Chris had helped drag her husband up to Mrs. Shafer's room at the hotel where they could talk in private, before heading toward the hot apple pie.

"Where's the boy?" he said after a long minute.

"He's down at the stables with that funny little man caring for the horses." She sat staring into her coffee for what seemed an eternity. Reverend Gibson cleared his throat before breaking the silence.

"And what did your husband have to say after we left?"

"That it was over. He wants a divorce. He believes that Mr. Baker and I have been living in sin. I tried to explain that he is simply a nice man, who helped us in our time of need, but he won't listen." She burst into tears, and Chris had suddenly lost his appetite for apple pie.

"I'm sorry he feels that way. There has been some talk, but anyone who knows you should know it simply isn't true," Mrs. Gibson said.

"I know, but he wouldn't listen. I tried...but he just called me names. Besides, I think he's only using that as an excuse. Looking back on things, I guess he never really wanted the responsibility of having a family." She blew her nose and tried to smile as she continued.

"We were both young, and he was so dashing...I just had to have him. But he still wanted to live a single life after we were married. He insisted on running with the same gang of rowdies night after night, gambling and doing whatever they did. He wouldn't hold a job or work our little piece of ground long enough to amount to anything. I guess if it wasn't the generosity of my own mother and father...and his, William and I would have more than likely starved long ago.

"When he said he wanted to come to California to seek his fortune, I agreed, thinking that somehow things might change. But they didn't. And I'm so ashamed and embarrassed." A sob escaped her throat as she covered her face. "My own husband doesn't want me or our children."

Chris couldn't recall many times in his life when he had felt genuine hatred, not even for the bluecoats during the war. They were just soldiers fighting for what they believed in, like every southern boy. He couldn't hate a man for doing his job, no matter how it might affect him personally. But he was feeling some mighty powerful things as he watched the preacher's wife put an arm around Mrs. Shafer.

"I reckon that make's him a true Yankee, because there ain't a southern boy that would do such a thing," he said, getting up from the table. "And I'd go teach him a lesson, except it'd only make things worser. If he wouldn't listen to the likes of a little lady like you, he certainly ain't gonna be listening to me."

"So, what do you plan to do now, my dear?" Reverend Gibson asked.

"Wait for a reply from my parents. Hopefully, they will send enough money for me to take my children back to New York. Then, I guess I'll give him his divorce. I don't see what else I can do."

"No, I don't guess there is anything else," the reverend said.

Chris headed toward the door, where he paused to shove his hat down on his head.

"Ma'am?" he said as he opened the door.

"Yes, Mr. Baker?"

"Reckon you'd mind if I take the boy with me for a few days? I plan on buying some cattle, and I suspect I might be needing myself another drover. I'll pay him fair wages."

She sat thoughtfully for a minute before answering. "No, Mr. Baker, I won't mind at all. I think it would be good for him to get away. It will keep his mind off....off what just happened."

"She will be fine, Mr. Baker," Mrs. Gibson said with a smile. "We have an extra room, and would be pleased if she moved in with us while she's waiting to hear from her parents."

"Yes, Ma'am. We will be leaving first thing in the morning. The boy and I'll fetch their things from the hotel and bring them over. If there's anything you need, be letting me know before then."

"Thank you, Mr. Baker. I certainly will."

Chapter 16

Johnny claimed he knew a man living near Tulare Lake named Mann, who had cattle he'd like to sell. Believing the Yokut had shown excellent judgment up to that point, Chris took Johnny and several members of his family with William, and headed south. The lake was fed by the Kings River, and it took the greater part of two days in reaching the river. Chris had a suspicion, about a day into the journey, that there had to have been someone closer willing to sell beeves, but that fact didn't seem to faze Johnny. He claimed that Mann's cattle were the best around, and that was where they should purchase their livestock.

The fact that they stopped each night at an Indian *rancheria* caused Chris to believe that the Indians were using the trip as an excuse to visit old friends and relatives. The folks they spent the nights with were friendly, and made quite a fuss over them being there. William seemed to blend right in with the Indian children, and even picked up some of their language, which was more than Chris could say for himself. He figured he was having enough trouble understanding that Yankee talk the boy's mother spoke, let alone any of the words Johnny's folks used.

When they finally reached the Kings River, they met more of Johnny's people, who were preparing to take an extended fishing trip downriver to the lake. The Indians had built a fifty foot long raft out of tules, which they called an *ah-aya*. They had used three bundles of tules, made separately and then bound together with one at the bottom, and two above, making sort of a keel boat. It had a

Poverty Flat

depression along the center of the deck where they had piled their dunnage. The way they had lashed the tules together reminded Chris of a big cigar, except the ends turned upward.

It seemed as though the Indians had most everything they needed stored on board, including mortars and pestles, baskets of acorns, acorn bread, seeds, meat, skins for bedding and an assortment of camping equipment. Chris first thought the thing might sink, but it seemed to float right nicely. When they got ready to launch, they posted eight or ten Indians on each side to man the poles, and asked him if he wanted to ride. Chris declined, using the excuse that he had better find a way to herd a bunch of cattle back upriver. Besides, he thought Bruiser looked a might safer than a bunch of river tules.

Johnny said the fishing trip, or *pah-ah-su*, was quite an annual event that everyone looked forward to. Chris discovered that Johnny's family weren't the only ones, because they met a number of Indians making the same journey, and some of them even swapped rides on each other's rafts. Chris bit his tongue as the trip moved at a snail's pace, taking ten days to reach the lake. The only thing keeping his temper in check was watching Johnny and his family. They seemed to be having the time of their lives, and the way William fit in seemed to make up for the loss of time.

Johnny explained that they had been making the trip most of their lives, and Chris noticed that several times, while camping along the river, some of the women dug up mortars and pestles that had been buried previously. They had designated hunters who would disappear during the day and show up at the camp each night carrying the fresh game they'd killed, and a couple came in with ducks they'd snared.

Chris had done quite a bit of fishing in his life, but had never seen anything resembling the gigging of fish that took place on the smaller rafts. The fisherman would lay on his stomach with his head and shoulders over a hole in the middle of the raft, which was covered with a tule mat, so he could see into the water without being seen by the fish. Then, when a nice-sized fish swam by, he would spear it with a cane gig. A group of Indians got William into the act, and his first fish was a small bass the size of the boy's hand and wrist put together.

"Mighty fine fish," Chris said as William displayed his catch. "But the way you was shouting, I thought you'd speared a whale. Aw, don't pay me no never-mind," he added and ruffled William's hair as the smile left the boy's face. "I was just joshing you some." Johnny said they planned on drying the meat and fish, and what they got on this trip would stock most of their food supply for the rest of the year.

The only thing Chris wasn't too sure about was how Mrs. Shafer would react when she learned about Johnny's family teaching her son to swim. Not that he thought there was anything wrong with a boy learning how to swim. Every child, in his opinion, should know how, and all the boys he grew up with were swimming in the creeks by the time they could walk. And the Indians had William swimming like a fish first day out. The thing was, Johnny's family swam in the altogether, every single one of them. And that's the way they taught William to swim. Seeing as how upstanding Mrs. Shafer was, Chris figured it might not be the smartest thing to mention. Not right away, anyhow.

Chris began to relax, and things were looking good, until they reached the lake.

******

They heard the mournful wailing long before reaching the clearing. Jacob Mann's adobe stood in the middle with the tack house and barn off to one side. The way things had been tossed around reminded Chris of Sheridan's march through Shenandoah, except they had left the house standing. Johnny ran past Chris and to the opposite side of the clearing where a small gathering of Indian women and two old men stood by an open grave. Chris told William to stay put and followed.

"Militia," Johnny said before he asked the question. "They came collecting Indians."

"Indians? What do they want with you folks?"

"They don't want us. And that's the problem. They want us all confined to a small reservation, and it doesn't matter that this was our land in the first place. And if anyone resists, they wind up like Mann." He nodded toward the grave.

"That feller's white," Chris said after taking a peek.

"Maggie was Wukchumne. They were married by a priest in San Jose, and had lived here almost five years. The militia came this morning and demanded the woman. Mann tried to explain that she was his wife, and he could take care of her. That didn't make any difference, and the leader ordered him to bring her out. When he refused, they knocked the door down and drug her outside. Mann tried to stop them, but they shot him in the back.

"They took his wife, and left him lying here," Johnny continued. "Some of my people were hiding in the bushes and they dug the grave. He was a good man, Chris."

Chris believed there was much to say about something like that, but didn't know how to put it into words. He had trouble thinking that these folks needed rounding up and carting off to a reservation in the first place. And anyone shooting a man in the front or the back for protecting his wife and family simply needed hanging. He helped with the burying and said a few words over him, asking God to protect Mann's wife and bring justice to the hydrophobied skunks that killed him.

Johnny said that Mann had some pretty good cattle back in the brush, and offered to take some men and round them up.

"Best not, son. Seeing as there's no way of paying for them, I think it best to leave them be. The way I figured, they still belong to that man's wife, and until she can come and claim what's rightfully hers, the Indians that's left should be taking care of them for her. We'd best be going."

He took William and Johnny, along with Cola'we and a couple of his cousins and made a beeline toward Hills Ferry. He left those that remained behind with orders to watch their backsides, knowing full well the skunks that killed Mann might still be lurking somewhere in the brush. They arrived three days later, stopping only long enough to sleep and get cleaned up before entering town. He left Johnny and his folks at the livery to care for the horses, and took the boy to see his mama.

It was Sunday morning, and Chris allowed William to sit beside his ma, while he took a spot on a log two rows back, not wanting to cause any more talk that might bring Mrs. Shafer hurt. Reverend Gibson, in Chris' opinion, was in fine fettle that morning. His subject happened to be gossip, and he proceeded to tell everyone how the hog got into the cabbage patch. He was starting to feel like his own backside had been scorched by the time the parson finished, although he couldn't remember the last time he was guilty of tongue-wagging.

******

It was over a second cup of coffee, after they had finished eating fried chicken at the reverend's house, that he told everyone about Jacob Mann. Both Mrs. Shafer and the preacher's wife had burst into tears by the time he had finished.

"They actually do things like that here in California? I can't believe it, and I'm from the south."

"Yes, sir, they certainly do," Reverend Gibson said, as he stirred his coffee. "It has been going on for years. This is what the politicians call *The Indian Question*. They have followed a *removal policy* set in order by our Federal Government, which simply means to move any Indian away from land white people might want. When they started, it was simple. They would drive them westward. The trouble is, here in California there is no westward. There's only ocean. So, about fourteen or fifteen years ago, Governor McDougal asked President Fillmore for federal aid. He claimed there were over 100,000 Indian warriors, all armed and ready for rebellion."

"I ain't seen nowhere near that amount of Indians, counting women and children," Chris said.

"There aren't. Anyway, Washington sent several agents to investigate the problem, and they presented what I believed might have been a fair proposal to the government. But, as you know, no one in Washington can seem to get together on anything. So, not much has happened. But now with the mad rush for gold, a great majority of the people coming here simply want the Indians to go away. There have been some newspapers calling for the complete extermination of Indians, and now that Governor Burnett is in office, *he's* even calling for extermination. The state has floated more than a million dollars in bonds to pay volunteers to, as he calls it, *suppress the Indian hostilities*, and one of the major newspapers says it has become a question of extermination now. They claim it is actually an act of mercy to exterminate them, because extermination would be saving white lives. The only kind of treaty these men want to see is one of bloodshed."

"We was poor folks, so we didn't have any slaves. But I knew of some who did, and I never knew them to treat their black folk like you're talking," Chris said. "What about Johnny Garcia and his folks? I got them working on my place. Any way of me stopping them from carting them folks off, or killing them?"

"Oh yes." The preacher snickered. "The state legislature passed a law saying that employed Indians are to be treated like property. But any unemployed Indian can be declared as vagrant and forced into labor. Of course, this has caused another problem for the Indians. It has become fairly profitable for some to go around kidnapping Indians, especially children. They can get paid for carting them off to the reservation, or killing them. And, in some cases, they get paid even more by selling them as servants or farm laborers. According to the way the law is written, if you happened to get angry with Johnny, you could beat the dickens out of him, or even kill him, and no one would say a word."

"What you've just told me is nothing less than plain murder. The state's paying folks to kill Injuns."

"I am afraid you're right, Mr. Baker. That's exactly what is happening. Fortunately, there are a few of us who are trying desperately to change things. But we're relatively few in number, and no one is listening."

"Maybe someone's gotta start things moving in the right direction. It might take awhile, but I'll mull things over."

******

It was three days later, and Chris had returned to Hills Ferry with Johnny and several members of his family to replenish his supplies, thinking he might make another attempt to go buy cattle. He left them at the livery while he visited the parson and checked on how Mrs. Shafer and the boy were doing. They were seated at the dining room table having coffee when there came a pounding at the door.

"Is Captain Baker here?" Reb almost knocked Mrs. Gibson over as he pushed his way inside.

"Yes, he's..." Reb ignored her and rushed into the dining room where they were seated. Chris caught a good look at the Colt .44 and shotgun he was toting as he scooted away from the table.

"Begging you women's pardon," he nodded politely toward Mrs. Gibson and Mrs. Shafer and touched the brim of his hat, "but I gotta see the Captain here. Better rustle outside, Cap, 'cause it's busting loose and there's gonna be hell to pay."

"Why, what's wrong?" Chris said grabbing his hat.

"Take your iron too." He grabbed Chris's forty-four from where he had hung it on the coat rack. "They got that Injun feller who was working for you and some of his family."

"Johnny? Where?" he said, strapping on the gunbelt.

"Right out there in the middle of town. They've got every one of them you left at the livery, including his sister, and they're right out there in the middle of town trying to sell 'em, big as brass." Chris grabbed his rifle from where it was leaning on the front porch and headed toward the center of town.

"They came in about a half-hour ago, wanting to leave their horses at the livery. When they seen the Injuns inside all hell broke loose. I tried telling 'em these folks was working for you, but they never paid me no mind. Anyway, Johnny, he puts up a pretty good fight, but three of them fellers jumped on top of him and like to beat the stuffings out of him, while the others held the other two boys at bay with their guns. Anyway, they're pretty liquored-up. I didn't think I'd have much luck stopping them by myself."

"You thought right," Chris said as they neared the crowd. "Better stay clear, Reb. I aim to inflict some pain, and might even do myself some killing, if need be."

"Hell, Captain. I never left your side during that fracas at Fredricksburg. What makes you think I'm going to do it now?" He hobbled off toward Chris' right and positioned himself near a watering trough. They had Johnny's hands tied behind his back and a rope around his neck. He looked as though he had been beaten half to death, then drug most of the way down the street. They had the rest tied with ropes around their necks like Johnny, and were in the process of selling Cola`we. A fat man in a fancy suit had a roll of money in his hand, and was fixing to make off with her as Chris approached. He took one look at Chris and quickly stuffed the money back in his pocket and scurried away.

"Excuse me," Chris' voice boomed. "You fellows seem to have made a big mistake. These folks are my employees. They are working for me on my ranch."

"Really," said one of the men seated on a bay. He was a big man with a red beard, and acted as though he really believed he was something. "Then why did we find them trying to steal horses down at the livery?"

"That's a lie and you know it. Those were my horses, and they were taking care of them. We just got back from Tulare Lake a couple of days ago, trying to buy cattle from Jacob Mann."

"Did you get any?"

"No, we found him dead. Some yellow coyotes looking to poach Indians, like you're trying to do, busted into his house and made off with his wife. And when he put up a tussle, they shot him in the back." This brought a rumble from the crowd and caused a couple of the poachers to look uncomfortable.

"You let that child go!" Mrs. Shafer burst through the crown, screaming. "Get that rope off her now! All of them!"

"Hell, it's that crazy lady," the young man who was holding Cola`we's rope said. He'd no more gotten the words out of his mouth when Mrs. Shafer snatched the rifle from Chris' hand. Remembering how she had scared the dickens out of him with the shotgun, he let her go, thinking she might do the same with these men. Instead, she shot the hat right off the man's head, then expertly injected another round into the chamber while keeping the gun pointed in his direction.

"I am not going to tell you again. I will shoot your head off if you do not untie that child this instant, and all the others, too."

"Now, lady," said the man on the bay. He had drawn his pistol and had it resting across the saddle horn. Chris had about decided to blow him into eternity when Mrs. Shafer spoke.

"William?"

"Yes, Ma'am?"

"I want you to count to three. And if that man doesn't put his gun away by the time you reach three, shoot him."

"Where, Ma?" He raised and cocked the Remington .32.

"Boy?" the red beard said.

"In the face. I don't care."

"Yes, Ma'am."

"Aw, come on lady. You can't have your boy..." the big man started.

"Start counting William."

"One..."

"Better do as she says, mister. That boy can shoot almost as good as his ma," Reb said, although Chris didn't believe he had any way of knowing the boy's shooting ability.

"Two..."

"Okay, okay," he said and holstered the gun. The man who'd lost his hat ran to untie Johnny and his relatives. Chris waited until the ropes were off Johnny before raising his voice.

"Johnny, which one of these skunks beat on you that away?"

It was Cola'we, his twelve-year-old sister who pointed toward the grinning visage of Frank Sorenson. Chris didn't know how he could have missed seeing him and his buddy, Bill. He felt his blood boil inside his head as he grabbed the Winchester from Mrs. Shafer's hand.

"Since when did you two give up being outlaws and start poaching Indians?"

"It's a living," Billy said.

"It's more like dying," he said, and moved closer. "Which one of you did the beating?"

"I did. What about it?" Frank said, and Chris shoved the rifle butt hard into his mouth, then whirled the gun around to where the barrel was pointed at Billy's chest.

"Please. Go ahead and pull that iron."

"Na-uh," he poked both hands in the air, "I ain't stupid enough to slap leather with you, Nails, even if you didn't have the drop on me. Besides, I wasn't the one who beat the boy, and I didn't shoot that man in the back either. That was Frank's doing. Honest."

Chris glanced at Frank as the man rolled over coughing and spit bloody teeth into the dirt.

"You tell him, and anyone else concerned. These folks are working for me. And I take it mighty personal when folks working for me are molested in any way." He then turned and yelled at the crowd gathered in the street.

"Anyone who touches anyone working on my place will have to answer to me. And I hope I don't have to, but I'll swear to Almighty God, I'll kill the first one who tries something like this again.

Chapter 17

The doctor said although Johnny should heal just fine, he would be laid up for a spell. Reb suggested it might be a good idea to have the Indians bed down inside his livery that evening where he could keep an eye out for them. That way Chris would be able to see to it they made it safely back to the ranch in the morning. He had been sitting quietly for the past hour inside the parson's house staring into the fireplace. Neither Mrs. Shafer nor William had said two words since the incident in the middle of the street. Pastor Gibson and his wife were busy trying to make everyone feel as comfortable as possible, but as far as Chris could tell, nothing was working.

One of the things Chris' mother had taught him was, never let anything troubling you rest until it's resolved, and if there wasn't any other way, meet it head on. Another thing he had learned from his days in the army was, if something seemed too big to swallow, laugh at it and it won't seem insurmountable. So, he began mulling over what had taken place in the street with Johnny and his folks, and burst out laughing. Everyone stopped what they were doing to stare at him as if he'd gone insane, which caused him to laugh harder. Then, after gaining control of himself, he toasted Mrs. Shafer with his coffee cup.

"Here's to you, Ma'am. If you scared them fellers half as much as you scared me this afternoon, I don't think they'll be causing anymore trouble."

"I certainly hope not. But I didn't find it in the least humorous, nor did I realize that I had frightened you, Mr. Baker. I didn't think anything would frighten you."

"Me? Why I've been scared spitless on more'n one occasion. Where'd you learn to shoot like that anyway?"

"I was raised on a farm, Mr. Baker. My father taught me how to shoot when I was a child."

"Then how come you pitched such a fit about my giving the boy a gun and having him learn how to use it?"

"Because, Mr. Baker," she paused as Mrs. Gibson refilled her cup with tea, "As I have already stated, I was afraid he might somehow get the idea that guns were a way of settling disagreements, and I wouldn't want that to happen. I was taught to shoot for sport and hunting…not killing another human being"

Chris couldn't contain himself and doubled over laughing.

"I don't see the humor in anything I said, Mr. Baker. Please enlighten us, so we can all laugh."

Everyone in the room, excluding her, was already laughing. Chris had no way of knowing if they were laughing at him, or what he saw as funny. After he had finally composed myself, he said, "You don't, huh?"

"No, I don't."

"Well, it was you using that Winchester, and the boy here fixing to shoot that man's nose off, that settled that little set-to this afternoon."

"I realize that. And I am totally ashamed of myself."

"Now, don't you go looking at things that way. If we hadn't gone out there and stopped them, Johnny and his family would all be slaves, or maybe dead, right this minute. And except for using guns, I don't really see how you could've handled it any other way. Those buzzards weren't gonna listen to you or me sweet talk them."

"I'm afraid Mr. Baker is right," Reverend Gibson said. "And they would not have stopped there. I don't really know for sure that they have stopped, but, perhaps they will leave the Garcia family alone. You were right in threatening them with violence."

"Thank you," she almost whispered.

"I'm just thankful you and your pa weren't wearing blue during the war," Chris said as she glared at him. "I'll tell you what, there weren't many of the Yankees I faced that could handle a gun like you did today. And we would've had us a real bad time, worser'n we did, if you were shooting at us."

******

Although Johnny insisted he felt well enough to travel, Chris decided to leave him at the ranch and took two of his cousins and William north, looking to buy cattle. They stopped at a couple of places, but Chris thought their beef critters were skinny little things and they didn't much impress him, so they kept following the river. It was in Grayson that Chris ran into Paco Morales.

"If you wanted cattle, *Señor*, why didn't you come see me first. The *Doña* has plenty of fat, lazy cattle, that are so tame you can pet them like a dog."

That sounded like sweet mountain music to Chris. After sending word to Hills Ferry, telling Mrs. Shafer her boy was fine and where they were going, he followed Paco northeast toward the gold country. The cattle Paco showed him were indeed big and fat, but they weren't lazy by any stretch of the imagination, and Chris thought they were as ornery as any Texas mossy-horn he had ever seen. He also knew they would have trouble getting them to the ranch.

"Just how many cattle are we talking about, *Señor*?"

He felt uncomfortable staring at the beautiful woman seated behind the desk. He knew Paco must have said something about her looks, but he'd expected to see an older woman, fifty to a hundred pounds overweight, with a sour disposition. Most of the people he had met, who had worked themselves up to having fancy titles, did so by stomping on those below them. But this girl seemed to be about the same age as Mrs. Shafer, and was prettier and nicer than a newborn colt. From what he could gather from talking to her *vaqueros*, she had earned her title by marrying her first husband, who'd gotten killed in some ruckus. But she had since married an Irish doctor, and had a two-year-old son full of spit and vinegar. And, from the looks of things, when she stood to shoo her rowdy son out of the office, she would have another one in a matter of months.

"Oh, I'm figuring on about a hundred head. That is, if you can spare that many."

"I think we might be willing to part with that many, Mr. Baker." She smiled. "And how much are you offering to pay for a hundred head of cattle?"

"Well, I've heard of prices ranging from $8.00, all the way to $40.00 a head since arriving in California.."

"*Si*," she nodded thoughtfully, "but I've also heard of some buyers paying as much as $75.00 a head in San Francisco."

"But seeing as we ain't in San Francisco, and I ain't planning on ever going there again, unless I absolutely have to, why don't you tell me what your beef critters are worth."

She burst out laughing and walked to the massive door leading to the hallway and clapped loudly. "Evangelina?" A young girl appeared almost magically.

"*Si, Doña* Kilkenney?"

"Tell *Señor* Hanky and my father I need them to show our guest around the rancho. And tell Julio to saddle Rudolfo's black for me. I would like to go with them."

"But *Doña*," the girl glanced at the slightly protruding belly, "your husband says…"

"Oh, pooh. I know what my husband says. But I want to go riding. Now, go do what I say."

The scolding was mild enough that the girl ran down the hall giggling. The woman ushered Chris into the kitchen before going upstairs to change. Maria, her portly maid, served coffee and had offered everything from homemade bread to a plate of beefsteak and beans by the time she returned in her riding gear.

******

Chris remarked that she had a right pretty hunk of land, and whistled when hearing it covered nearly seventy square miles. From what he could tell, the folks working there were mostly Mexican and Indian with a few white folk tossed into the mix. They were right friendly enough, but Chris had a suspicion that a few like Paco, Juan, and the old grizzled ex-Texas Ranger called Hanky, were not someone you would want to cross. And it didn't take long for him to decide the woman who owned the place was a piece of art herself. Her pa was a retired general in the Mexican Army and had a right smart operation going. But Chris got the feeling, as the afternoon wore on, that she was the one running the whole shebang. And the way she mounted that black Arabian, being pregnant and all, and rode several miles, caused him to think she wasn't one to be trifled with either.

Her doctor husband was waiting, and fit to be tied when they arrived back to the house. He started to give her the what-for for going horseback riding while being with child, but, being the woman she was, she simply smiled and gave him a little kiss on the cheek, then went about her business.

They insisted on having a celebration in honor of their guests, that included music and dancing and roasting several critters over an open-pit fire in the patio. The *Doña* laughed when Chris remarked that the chilies and beans were hot enough to take the hair off your tongue, if you had any. Chris used the hot chilies as an excuse for choking as Paco introduced his beautiful wife he'd been bragging about. She turned out to be a skinny little girl with long, stringy blond hair and freckles. Chris shook her hand and joked about her marrying an ugly cowboy like Paco, as the *vaquero* beamed with pride. Chris decided she was a nice girl, just not what he had expected after listening to him the several days they spent on the trail. But it was easy to see they loved each other, so he guessed that's what counted.

Chris decided that William might be the lucky one. Being the spitting image of his ma, the boy had taken the eye of a smart-looking girl about his age named Olga. She latched onto him like a burr and drug him all over that patio. Chris had no idea if they understood each other, since the girl talked in rapid Spanish, and William answered in Yankee English, but he decided they must be communicating in some fashion. The girl had him in the middle of the patio dancing by the time Chris drifted inside to talk business.

******

"To be honest, the cattle prices have been dropping," she said, drumming her fingers against her desk. "They have fallen from approximately $40.00 to as low as $16.00 in some instances, and that has put a huge burden on many of the ranchos. Because of the debt imposed on us by having to prove ownership in court, many owners have had to sell their property. Or, in some cases, the banks simply foreclose and take the land."

"Yes, Ma'am. I've heard something about that."

"But, that is none of your concern," she said with a sweep of her hand, as though she were shooing a fly. "What you want to know is cattle prices."

"Yes, Ma'am."

"We have been lucky enough to have a year-round water supply on *Rancho Manantial Escondido*. Therefore, our cattle are well fed, as you can see. I think a price of $18.00 a head might seem fair, considering the condition of the animals you will be buying."

"How does $25.00 delivered sound? I ain't got but me, the boy and a couple of Indians. And after seeing them old mossy-horns, I know there ain't no way of us getting

Poverty Flat

them off your land, let alone to Poverty Flat. Besides, I should be getting that boy back home to his ma. She'll be mighty worried by now."

"Poverty Flat? Doesn't sound like much of a place to raise cattle," Hanky said.

"No, it's pretty good, actually. Poverty Flat's what the boy's ma calls her place. It borders up next to mine, where I got plenty of fresh water. Both places have good grass. We'll do fine."

"I think we might be able to get your cattle to you, *Señor*." She looked at a tall young man who was seated on her sofa rolling a cigarette.

"Perhaps you could take Juan and Paco and a few Indians and make the drive, *Señor* Tex?"

"Maybe," he said lighting the cigarette. "It'll take us a few days to round that many up. How're we supposed to know where to take 'em, without you being along?"

"I'll leave the Yokuts I brung along. They probably know the way better than I do. But there's one thing I need to warn you about. I've had me a little set-to with some Indian hunters around Hills Ferry. You'd best keep your eyes peeled if you're planning on keeping your Indian vaqueros"

"Yeah, we've seen a few of 'em nosing around here too," Hanky said.

"How'd you handle it?" Chris was hoping to find some new magical way of protecting his drovers without blowing someone's head off.

"We gave a few of them bright new crosses out near the river," Tex said. "Now, they leave us alone."

******

"That girl, Olga? She kissed me," William said as Chris was beginning to doze off.

The celebration had lasted into the wee hours of the morning, and he was dead tired. The fact was, there was someone in the patio that minute, strumming a guitar and singing at the top of his lungs. Chris thought he had a nice voice, but a man needed his sleep. The boy had something on his mind, so he rolled over and studied him in the darkness.

"That so?"

"Yeah."

"Where'd she kiss you? On the cheek?"

"No, on the mouth."

"Hmm. Maybe she likes you. What'd you think of it?"

"I don't know. At first, I thought it was kind of yucky, but then it kind of excited me too. You won't tell mom, will you?"

"I don't know, son. I think a man's first kiss should be something his mother needs to know about. But I don't think she's gonna get mad at you, if that's what you're worried about. And, as far as feeling all mixed up inside, I reckon that's a woman's job to make a man feel that way. The question is, do you like this Olga?"

"I don't know. Yeah, in a way. She's real nice and all that. But she giggles a lot and wouldn't leave me alone."

"She's a girl, boy. Womenfolk do that sort of thing. What'd y'all talk about?"

"I don't know. I couldn't understand her most of the time."

"Well, now, that ain't such a bad thing. Most men don't understand what a woman's saying half the time anyway. That's only natural. But yes," he said yawning, "I'd say you're mixed up alright. So, don't worry none, son. It'll turn out okay in the end."

He was quiet for a long time, and Chris decided he'd finally gone to sleep, when he sat up in the middle of the bed.

"Does ma make you feel that way?"

"What's that, son?"

"All mixed up inside. Does ma make you feel that way?"

"Well, I reckon she does."

"Why?"

"You're full of all sorts of questions, aren't you boy? She makes me feel that way partly for the same reason you feel about Olga. But I'd be hard pressed telling you everything. Like I said, they're women, and that's their job. Now, let's try and get some sleep."

******

They were up early feasting on plates of beef steak, potatoes, beans, eggs and tortillas. Chris washed his down with several mugs of hot coffee while William had milk. He paid the woman in full for her cattle, and she gave him a written bill of sale and a promise they would be delivered in a matter of weeks. They said their goodbyes and he spied William giving the girl a peck on the cheek before climbing the corral railing to mount his pony. He looked like a cat who'd just eaten the fattest rat, so Chris acted as though he hadn't noticed the kiss. They rode in silence most of the morning until he finally broke his self imposed silence.

"Yeah, I think I do like her."

"I'd say so." Chris nodded. They rode like two men headed toward destiny. A little mixed up, but they'd find whatever it was sooner or later.

Things were looking mighty good, and Chris was making plans for some changes he wanted to make once the cattle arrived. They checked themselves into the Grayson Hotel before Chris decided he had better send a wire, letting Mrs. Shafer know they were on their way. He had just handed the operator his note, when he said a telegraph had arrived for Chris two days earlier. It simply read:

Mr. Christian Baker (stop) please come quickly (stop) something terrible has happened.

Reverend Robert Gibson

Chapter 18

Some people parcel things into little boxes, saying one thing is better than the next, or that this isn't as bad as that thing over there. Chris reckoned that that belief might be true, except he had a tendency to believe bad news is bad news, no matter how you slice it. Of course one might say that certain things are worse than others, and he reckoned that was also true. A man who's just lost his favorite hound isn't as bad off as someone who's lost his favorite horse. And neither of them were as bad off as someone who's lost their ma or pa, or someone else close to them. But he had no way of knowing what the *something terrible* in Reverend Gibson's telegram was, even after sending a cable to the preacher asking what was wrong, because he didn't receive any reply. They were both worried half-sick by the time they reached Hills Ferry, and rode right up to the Reverend's front porch. Chris was fixing to pound on the door when Mrs. Shafer busted through to engulf William in her arms and cover his dusty face with kisses.

"I'm sorry," she said, pulling him over to sit on the porch, "but I'm afraid I have some terrible news, William. Your father is dead."

Chris took a long look at the boy crying on his mother's shoulder before following Velma Gibson inside.

"I'm sorry, I didn't get your telegram until this morning, " Reverend Gibson said, as his wife poured the coffee. "You see, we had taken Mrs. Shafer to Stockton to claim the body, and didn't get back until early this morning. We've been holding the remains in the warehouse at the

Poverty Flat

dock, hoping you and William would arrive in time for the funeral."

"How'd it happen?" he said over a sip of coffee.

"According to what we heard, he got into an argument over a card game and attacked another player. Some of the witnesses claimed Mr. Shafer was getting the worst of it and tried reaching for his gun. I guess the other gambler was much quicker with a knife. It will certainly be a closed-coffin funeral," he added after, blowing across his steaming mug.

"How's the missus taking it?"

"Surprisingly well," Velma said. "Oh, she cried some, when the news first arrived, and a little when we claimed the body. But the worse actually came when it was time to telegraph his family back east. Don't you think so, Robert?"

"Yes, I had to send the wire myself. I left out most of the details, mind you. I simply said he had passed away in an accident. May God forgive me for lying."

"Well, folks don't need to know everything."

He excused himself and went to join them on the porch. Chris had known folks who try to think of fancy words to say at times like this, thinking they'll somehow make the grieving person feel better. But in his experience, there's times a man didn't need to go jawing. What was important was he'd be there, and that was what he was intending to do. He sat, with the boy in the middle, watching folks wander up and down the street, just being there. It seemed like an eternity before the boy excused himself and went inside.

"You've got yourself a fine boy, Mrs. Shafer. He handled himself like a man the whole time we were gone. You ought to be proud of him."

"I am, Mr. Baker. Thank you."

"I'm sorry to hear about your man. It must be real hard on you."

"Thank you again, but no, not like you think," she said with a weak smile. "I know you might consider it strange that I'm not crying and carrying on, but my husband died a long time ago."

"Ma'am?"

"I did my mourning over the years we were together. Every time he had a fling with another woman, or gambled away what money we had, or abandoned us for weeks on end. And yes, it was hard." Her voice trembled and she dabbed her eyes with a laced handkerchief.

"As far as I'm concerned, Mr. Baker, I held George's funeral inside my room at the hotel, when you beat him and forced him to see me. That is why you don't see me carrying on. And please don't feel ill toward me if I don't shed tears over his grave. If I do cry, and God forgive me for feeling this way, it will be for his family in New York. They really are nice people, and I love them. I hope you can understand."

"Yes, Ma'am. I believe I do understand. I'm just sorry you've had so much trouble in your life. And I'm sorry that Edith and the boy ain't got a father they can look up to."

"Yes, I'm sorry about that also, Mr. Baker."

******

He reckoned the funeral was as nice as one can be for a reprobate who deserted his family. He certainly didn't shed any tears over George Shafer's coffin, and the only prayer he uttered was for the missus and her children. Then, leaving the boy with his mama, Chris excused himself, saying he needed to get back to the ranch and see how things were going. He was busy at the livery saddling Bruiser, when Reb eased up to his side.

"You remember that feller you whupped, Frank Sorenson?"

"Ain't likely to forget him. Why?"

"Because he's back in town asking questions about you."

"Well, he knows where to find me, if he really wants to."

"He's also been hinting that you somehow got all that money you've been throwing around illegal-like."

"You don't believe that, do you Reb?"

"Me? You know better'n that, Captain. I'd say if there was anything illegal going on, it was them doing the doing, not you."

"You've got that right. I ran into them awhile back on the road to Columbia. They were riding with Ingram back then."

"Rufus Ingram?"

"That's the one."

"Now that's more'n a poke in the eye. He's about as rotten as any Yankee you'd run into."

"Worse. They were planning to keep the war going, and wanted me to join up with them. They had some crazy plan of robbing stages and pirating ships to support their effort. Craziest danged thing I'd ever heard of. The only question I have is what happened to their plan, and why are those two idjits back in town?"

"Well, for one thing," Reb chuckled, "they got the hell shot out of themselves."

Chris stopped adjusting the cinches to listen.

"Simon, over at the general store, says he heard that they did stick up two Concord coaches from Virginia City that were headed for Placerville. They got away with some $26,000.00 from one, and another $700.00 from the other near Carson City. I guess they were living pretty high and mighty, until Sheriff Hall of San Jose cornered them on a ranch near the Salinas River. The posse shot the dickens out of Ingram's gang. Killed one of them outright, hung a feller named Poole, and got one more locked up in jail. Ingram and a feller named Baker got away. But last anyone heard of them, they was headed for Missouri."

"And we're lucky enough to get Frank Sorenson and Billy Grant."

"You said it. But seeing as he's laying for you, you'd better watch out, Captain."

"I ain't expecting him to be much trouble." He gave the cinches one final tug and climbed into the saddle.

"Maybe not. But I'll bet you this livery against the buggy that you'll have to kill that boy before this is over."

"You might be right, Reb. But I hope not."

******

Johnny's wounds were healing fine, and they had the place looking right pretty when Chris arrived. They'd also finished building a dam across the creek, and a passel of naked children were having the time of their lives splashing around in the pond. The corrals were up, the bunkhouse mostly finished, with a pot of flowers sitting in the middle of the dining room table.

"We thought the woman might be returning with you," Johnny said.

"Mrs. Shafer? No, she's got troubles enough of her own. Her husband went and got himself killed while we were gone."

"That makes things easier for you."

"Huh? What are you talking about?"

"The woman. Now you can marry her and bring her out here to stay."

"Aw, you're loonier than a locoweed-fed mule. She ain't interested in marrying the likes of me. Besides, she's a Yankee, and she's headed back home to her folks where she belongs."

"Has she left?"

"No. She wrote her folks, and now she's waiting for them to send her the money."

"Why didn't you give her the money, if you have no interest in her?"

That was one question Chris had never considered. It wasn't that he didn't have the money to give. That was

Poverty Flat

something he could have done long ago if he had wanted to. But seeing as the thought had never crossed his mind, Chris stood staring at the grinning Yokut.

"I say you love the woman and don't want her to leave."

"You're crazy."

"Think so? I'll ask my father to get the grizzly hide and hold ceremony. He'll ask the spirits and they will tell us what you should do."

"I thought you didn't believe in such things."

"I don't. But I'll give it a try, if it will help you to make up your mind."

******

Considering they had the place in such good shape, there wasn't much for Chris to do until the cattle arrived. After fidgeting and getting into the Indian's way for a few days, Chris decided to head back to Hills Ferry on Saturday to check on Mrs. Shafer and see how the boy was doing. Besides, he reasoned, it gave him an excuse to get away from that smart-alec Yokut who thought he knew everything. Johnny had talked his father into holding some sort of Indian ceremony with dancing and chanting that lasted well into the night. Chris tried telling them he was a Baptist, and didn't cotton to such goings-on. But just like Mrs. Shafer, they ignored him and kept on with their ceremony. Johnny informed Chris the next morning that his father had come to the conclusion that Mrs. Shafer was supposed to be his woman and that he should bring her and the children out to the ranch to live. Chris told him they were all crazy, and that bringing her out there would only add one more crazy person to the ranch and drive him insane, if he wasn't already there.

He was giving Bruiser a rubdown in one of the stalls, when Reb ambled up close to say trouble was brewing.

"Yes sir, that Sorenson feller's got half the town believing you're some sort of Jessie James, who's robbed everyone from here to Missouri."

"That so? And what do you think, Reb?"

"Me? I just think he's looking to get himself kilt."

"You don't believe I'm a bandit, then?"

"Naw, Captain. Iffin' you or me either one was a thief, we could've taken all sorts of payroll and what-not back during that Yankee aggression. We was always around some sort of pot of gold, and we never touched one cent that didn't belong to us."

"Much obliged, Reb," he said, clapping him on the shoulder. "Coming from you that means a lot."

Chris headed down the street at a brisk walk, noticing that folks treated him kind of queer. Some that he had become acquainted with the over the past couple of months turned their backs when they saw him coming. Others acted like they didn't see him, and the few that spoke weren't friendly at all. He guessed the parson's talk last Sunday hadn't been heeded by anyone. Of course only a handful had been on hand to hear it in the first place. By the time he reached Simon Newman's store Chris was starting to feel uncharitable, and hoping to run into Frank Sorenson.

"Yes, it is true. He has somehow spread enough rumors that some doubt about your honesty has taken hold." Simon gave Chris a firm nod from where he stood behind the counter.

"And how do you feel?"

"I'd say you would have had to stick up a lot of banks and stages to have the money you've been spending lately. But then, it doesn't matter much what I believe now, does it? Look," he continued as he poured two cups of coffee, "this is a small community. And most of these people arrived hoping to get rich and few have. If the truth were known, most have less than what they came with. They are angry and greedy, and hate to admit that someone else has somehow discovered a way to get rich, even if that person did it through a lot of hard work. They are going to believe the worse about you, until you prove them wrong."

Up to that point Chris hadn't thought too much about the money he had been spending. Outside of buying that hunk of land and the cattle, he'd never figured it to be a lot. But he *had* stayed in the hotel most of two months, and *had* paid for Mrs. Shafer and her two children. And they had eaten their meals at restaurants and he bought the team and buggy. Of course, Reb had almost given it away, so he would have been a fool not to buy them. Then they had taken that trip down river and he built a ranch house, bunkhouse and all that went with it. He guessed it did look like he owned a gold mine. And he'd been a fool in the process. Not for what he had done, but for the way he'd handled things.

"Thanks, Simon. You've helped me see the light." Chris set the empty cup on the counter and turned to leave when he heard Simon's voice behind him.

"Wait! How did you get the money, Chris?"

"You'll find out soon enough. Just as soon as everyone else does."

Seeing no one on the street who wanted to talk to him, Chris made a beeline for Parson Gibson's house. It was Mrs. Shafer who answered his knock, and she didn't look too friendly either. In fact, in Chris's opinion, she was downright rude when she got in his face jawing, before he even got inside.

Chapter 19

An angry Yankee female was the last thing Chris needed, and seeing as he wasn't in any mood to be trifled with, he decided to jaw back a little.

"I don't see as how I got a Jack penny is any of your concern, Ma'am. It ain't like we're married or nothing."

"No, I can thank God for that, Mr. Baker. But you've spent a lot of money on us, and I believe I deserve the right to know where that money came from."

"You do now?" He could see the ashen face of Velma Gibson staring at them from the living room. She had her hands on William's shoulders. "And just what makes you think you, or anyone else in this berg, deserves to know anything about me?"

"Because if that money was tainted in anyway it will reflect on the reputations of me and my children."

"Well, I'm sorry to have soiled y'all's good names. I only seen that y'all needed some help, and I was trying to be Christian-like. But, seeing as how you didn't appreciate it none, I'll be leaving. Sorry to have offended you, Ma'am." He touched the brim of his hat and finished by slamming the door.

What had started out to be a fairly nice day kept going from bad to worse. The man at the hotel refused to give Chris the key to his room, as the owner had ordered him not to take any more money from him until he could prove it wasn't stolen.

"I'm terribly sorry, Mr. Baker, but he's afraid that the law would make him pay it back, and he's already accepted a sizable amount of money from you. I hope you can understand."

"Yeah, I understand alright. An old southern boy like me can understand a lot of things. For starters, I can understand who my friends are."

"Oh, but it isn't that way, Mr. Baker."

"Sure it is, Harold. Anybody who'd take the word of an outlawing Indian poacher like Frank Sorenson over a feller who pays his bills and works hard at making life better for those around him, ain't no friend of mine. I'll find me someplace else to bunk for the night."

But he found it wasn't much better anywhere he went, so Chris wound up at the livery eating biscuits and beans.

"This here's right tasty grub. Much obliged, Reb," he said, washing down a mouthful with a swig of coffee.

"It sure beats some of that stuff they cooked up near the end of the war, anyway. Say," he pointed at Chris with his fork, "what do you reckon that was old Henry Jones gave us that time just before Christmas. I know he said it was wild turkeys, but it didn't taste like no turkey I ever ett."

"Buzzard would be my guess."

"Ha! I never thought about buzzards, but I'll bet you're right. There was sure plenty of them hanging around our battlefields. Anyway, whatever they was, I was hungry enough I was figuring them to be mighty tasty."

"Mind if I bed down here for the night, Reb?"

"Mind? No, you can sleep anywhere you want. In one of the stalls, or right over there on the floor." He pointed to the opposite wall in his tiny office with his fork. "It don't make me no never-mind. I don't care where you sleep."

They had just scrubbed out their plates and Chris was starting to unroll his gear when they heard a commotion in the street.

"Better come here, Captain," Reb said, peering out the door. "Looks like Chancellorsville all over again."

"What the…?" Chris stared at the crowd. It seemed half the town had gathered in the street, but he didn't care a hoot about most of them. The first face he saw was that of Frank Sorenson. Chris snatched the Winchester from where it was leaning against the wall and readied himself, when a tall, lean fellow eased his way through the crowd and toward the doorway. Chris had seen him before, and he had a silver star on his vest.

"Is Christian Baker inside?" he said politely to Reb.

"Yes, sir. Come on in, but the rest of these fellers will have to stay outside. I ain't got much room in here."

"That's fine. It's none of their concern anyway." He came in and Reb closed and barred the door.

"A little out of your jurisdiction, ain't you Tom?" Chris said, and leaned the rifle back against the wall.

"Maybe, but Dick Purvis is kind of busy with a couple of saloon shootings in Modesto, and seeing as how two of those robberies were in San Joaquin County, he said he wouldn't mind my asking you a few questions."

"I wouldn't mind either, if I knew anything about them. But seeing as I don't, I think you've simply wasted a lot of valuable time."

"Perhaps, but there's been some talk about you being involved. Any truth in that, Chris?"

"Nope, but it doesn't seem to make any difference now, does it?"

"How do you mean?"

"Well, me and a couple of Mexican drovers seen the feller who's been doing most of the talking awhile back up near Columbia. Him and another feller was hanging mighty close to Rufus Ingram. I take it you've heard of him?"

"Yes, I know all about Captain Ingram. Go on," Tom said, taking a seat near Reb's potbellied stove.

"Well, they was wanting me to join up in that crazy scheme of theirs to take over Mexico. But I told them it was the dumbest thing I'd ever heard of. Even the Mexicans I was riding with thought so. Well, I guess I offended them, 'cause they rode off and wouldn't even join us for a sociable cup of coffee."

"It was the craziest thing I've heard of myself," Tom said, laughing. "Okay, I can believe that. Now what about all this money you're supposed to have? Where'd it come from?"

"Well, let's just say I had it when I came here."

"That won't do Chris. You know me better that that. There's been close to $34,000.00 taken, and I'd like to know where your money came from."

"Well, if you'd asked Simon at the general store, you'd find I gave him a bank draft for that land he sold me, and I gave that Mexican woman another draft for $2,500.00 when I bought her cattle. Now you tell me, when have you ever known a thief to put his money in a bank?"

"You got me there, Chris. I never have." He grinned and leaned forward in his chair so his face was close to where Chris was seated. "But I still don't see what the big secret about where you got your money is. I'm going to keep pestering until you tell me."

"There ain't no secret to it. I just ain't told no one, because I didn't think it was any of their business. I didn't come here bragging about having a little poke stashed away, because I ain't the type that likes to go around bragging no matter how much money I got. When everyone started believing that skunk out in the street, instead of trusting me, I just figured I wasn't gonna tell them nothing at all. They can just go climb a pole for all I care."

"Okay, I can't say as I blame you any. But I still need to know where a cowpuncher like you came up with whatever amount of money you have, so I can clear your name."

"Fair enough," Chris said, and tore a blank page out of Reb's ledger book. He grabbed a stub of a pencil and started scribbling. "Telegraph this feller at the bank in Denver and tell him I said it's okay to tell you what you need to know. Then ask away. He knows where every dime came from." Chris folded and handed him the paper.

"Okay, I'll get busy on it right away." He stuffed the paper in his shirt pocket. "But you might consider telling a few of these folks, especially that Preacher and Mrs. Shafer. They are mighty worried and are supposed to be your friends."

"I thought so too. But the way she lit into me earlier when I went to visit, I don't plan on explaining nothing to her. Besides, I thought friends were supposed to be trusting one another, not accusing them of being thieves."

"Suit yourself," the sheriff stood to tower over Chris, "but if I was you, I think I'd change my mind a little about telling certain folks. Life can get mighty lonely for a man if he doesn't have any friends, especially when he's fixing to settle down and build himself a home."

Chris waited until he had opened the door before asking, "Am I under arrest?"

"No, I ain't got nothing to arrest you on yet. Just hang around close until I get some answers. Seeing as it's Saturday, I don't expect that there's anybody around the bank in Denver, so I probably won't be getting any answers until sometime Monday or Tuesday, if even then."

"Well, that might be putting a kink into things. I'm supposed to be receiving cattle out at my place right soon, and I'd like to be there to do it."

"Can't be helped, Chris. If you'd been more honest and helpful with folks from the start, maybe none of this talk would have taken root. Just don't leave town until I get some answers, or I *will* toss your carcass into the slammer."

He closed the door and Chris sat cogitating things. Tom Cunningham was smart, and he was probably right about Chris' being too secretive. Chris had been trying to act like a humble Christian, and turned out acting like a thief. He had also turned out being a great image for a young man like William to follow. Now he was stuck inside a livery, sleeping on the floor with a hundred head of cattle coming

Poverty Flat

and couldn't even be there when they came. Fine rancher he was going to make.

"What are you going to do, Captain?" Reb said, handing him a cup of coffee.

"Well, as I see it, I ain't got much choice but to sit right here and wait. Reckon I ought to go over and try explaining things to the parson and Mrs. Shafer tomorrow?"

"I would, if it was me."

******

Chris parked his carcass on one of the log pews early the next morning before anyone arrived for Sunday meeting, thinking he might get a chance to explain a few things before a crowd gathered, but it didn't turn out that a way. There were several families already perched atop logs by the time Reverend and Mrs. Gibson arrived with the Shafers in tow. Most of the worshipers, especially Mrs. Shafer, treated him like he had the plague, and Chris was beginning to feel mighty low by the time the meeting was over. He hung around hoping for a chance to talk, but Mrs. Shafer brushed past, ramrod stiff, without speaking. Then Chris began to get good and mad.

"Mr. Baker, Mr. Baker," he heard Velma Gibson yelling, as he stomped out of the congregating area.

"Ma'am?" he said as she scurried to catch up.

"I was hoping you could join us for Sunday dinner. I have an extra place already set, and a platter of fried chicken."

"Sounds mighty tempting, Ma'am, but I'd best be declining. It seems my presence is making some folks uncomfortable around here. But I would be liking to speak to you and the Reverend and Mrs. Shafer to let y'all know what's been on my mind."

"I think that can be arranged," she said, taking him by the arm. "Then, we shall discuss that chicken dinner."

They left the preacher talking to a couple about their upcoming marriage, and headed toward their house. Velma Gibson seemed downright pleasant, and ignored the curious glances of the people they passed as she held onto Chris' arm. But Mrs. Shafer acted as though the minister's wife had brought Lucifer home when Chris entered the door.

"What is he doing here?"

"I brought him, Mary." Velma Gibson was about as cool as Chris had seen any woman. "He's my guest in my own house, and says he has something to tell us. Then, we shall sit down and have a pleasant dinner."

"I don't believe he has anything to say that I'd be interested in hearing."

"Yes, Ma'am, I think I do," Chris said. "And I'm hoping you'll listen, because I probably won't be staying for chicken dinner."

"Alright, Mr. Baker. What is it you have to say?"

"Well, first of all, I'd like to be asking a favor of you."

"I doubt that I'll be accommodating Mr. Baker, but what is your request?"

"Well, I might have several requests, and one of them being that you quit acting so high and mighty. I come here in peace."

"Fine," she said with a curt nod, "I'll grant that wish. Ask away."

"Well, I'd like the boy to ride out to the ranch and tell them Indians I won't be coming home for a few days and they'll have to handle things."

"No, I can't let that happen."

"And why not? It's kind of important. I've got cattle coming."

"It's too long of a ride and too dangerous for someone his age."

"Oh, but Ma'am, he handles himself like a man. Besides, he could ride Bruiser and make that ride in one day."

"That's only part of the problem, Mr. Baker. I won't allow William to be associated with someone who might be...a thief, or even worse, until this is all settled. It would sully his reputation."

Chris felt as though another burr had been placed under his saddle, and didn't know whether to laugh or cry. So, he decided to do neither.

"Well, it's kind of late for that, isn't it? The whole blamed town's been seeing y'all hanging around with me for most of two months now. Besides, he ain't gonna be with me. If he needs someone to tag along, he can be taking Reb."

"He would still be doing you a favor by going to your ranch. Which reminds me," she paused to rummage around in her handbag and came out with two gold coins, "I believe these belong to you."

"No, Ma'am. They belong to the boy. That was his wages for helping me buy cattle."

"No, you might as well take it, because I won't allow him to have it...not until we can settle on where it came from."

"It came from me."

"That's exactly what I mean. It might be stolen."

"I'm sorry you feel that way, Ma'am." he took the coins and tossed them in his hand. He could see the boy standing dejected in the kitchen doorway and it made him all the angrier.

"When I first showed up on your doorstep that night a few months ago, I was just a cowboy looking to get in out of the rain. I didn't give two hoots in a holler about you and would've ridden on, except I seen you was in a bad way. So I hung around, trying to help you out some. And I really did try finding that husband of yours, no matter what anyone thinks. I'm sorry if I caused you and the boy any trouble, because that's not what I intended. And I'm real good and sorry you feel the way you do about me, Ma'am." He slammed the coins down on top of the little table by the door.

"There's your wages, son. If your ma won't let you keep it, give it to the church. 'Cause I ain't no thief, and I won't be stealing wages from nobody who works for me." Chris jerked open the door, but paused at her voice behind him.

"Where did you get all the money you've been spending, Mr. Baker?"

"I don't see how that concerns you, Ma'am, seeing as you already have your mind made up about me. Ask your boy. He's known where I got it from the first day I met you."

Chapter 20

He stormed out the door wondering how any one person could be warm and friendly one minute and colder than a blizzard in the Rockies the next, but decided that must be a Yankee trait of some sort. It wouldn't have surprised him any to discover they trained their youngsters to be that way from the time they were little. He also reckoned he was madder than a wet hen, and ignored Velma Gibson when she yelled for him to wait. Chris instead shucked a trail toward the livery and grabbed his grip out of Reb's office. He was in the process of saddling Bruiser when Velma entered the doorway flushed, with sweat glistening on her brow.

"I wish you would reconsider leaving, Mr. Baker. Mary didn't really mean to say those hateful things."

"She didn't, huh? Well, it's like this, Mrs. Gibson," he paused after tossing the saddle blanket across Bruiser's back and stared at her, "I never figured a person said much that wasn't already inside them, so she must've been thinking I'm a thief for her to say those things. Now, that must make some sort of sense to you, doesn't it?"

"Yes, and I quite agree with you, but..."

"There ain't no buts about it, Ma'am. She was more than willing to accept my help when she needed it. But now, she don't want her boy to be associated with me, 'cause she considers me an outlaw and thinks it will look bad. Well," he paused as he tossed the saddle on Bruiser's back, "that's fine, because the way I see it, she ain't got no ties on me whatsoever. And I ain't got none on her either. I helped her out in her time of need without expecting anything in return, and that's what I got. So, we're square as far as I'm concerned."

"I just hate to see you run off with bitter feelings toward someone. It's not like you, Mr. Baker."

"Now, why would you be so concerned about me and my feelings when half this town wants to see me hang?"

"My husband and I are not like *half this town*. We have gotten to know you, and happen to like you. And I also know that it's not like you to hold a grudge."

Reb came though the back door and tossed his pitchfork into one of the empty stalls. He wiped his brow with a dirty neckerchief and snorted.

"Now, where's this idjit think he's going?" he said to Mrs. Gibson.

"I didn't ask him. He's angry and won't listen to reason."

"That so, Captain?"

"I ain't got no reason to be hanging around here, Reb. Besides nobody wants me in town, so I don't see as it's any concern to anyone where I go."

"Well, now you're wrong on a couple points there, Captain, if you don't mind me saying so."

"Now, how's that?" Chris squared around to face him, but Reb didn't budge one inch. He surprised Chris by getting in his face.

"First of all, several folks want you around, regardless of what the rest say."

"Tell me who, if you're so smart."

"Me, the preacher and this woman," he nodded toward Mrs. Gibson, "Simon at the store... I could keep going if you want me to. But seeing as *where* you're going is a real big point with that sheriff, I'd have second thoughts about leaving town, if I was you. That temper of yours might get you into bigger trouble than you're already in."

Chris hated to admit it, but the little man was making sense. And seeing as he didn't have any desire to be locked inside some cell for something he didn't have any part in, he pulled the saddle back off Bruiser and hung it over the stall railing.

"Alright, but don't expect me to be coming around your place anytime soon," he snapped at Velma. "That woman staying there has herself a real case of Yankee pride that she needs to deal with."

"You both do, Mr. Baker," she said with a grin, as she turned away. "Only yours happens to be southern pride, and it might be just a little worse."

Chris hadn't cussed in so long he didn't think he could remember the words. But he considered Velma Gibson was one preacher's wife he really wanted to give a cussing to. He jerked the blanket off Bruiser and stomped around the livery, throwing things against the wall.

"Here, now," Reb yelled. "If ya got yourself so much energy, why not take it out on something constructive?" He tossed Chris a shovel. "The stalls need mucking out."

******

He was laying in a hammock strung across Bruiser's stall, when Tom Cunningham strolled through the door Wednesday afternoon.

"Now, that's the life," he said, all jolly like he was talking to an old friend.

"Not when you've got things that should be getting done."

"Well, your story checks out for the most part."

"And what part doesn't check out?" Chris said, rolling out of the hammock and onto his feet.

"You got your money just like you said you did. But there's a woman working in a restaurant in Jamestown that claims to have seen you with Rufus Ingram not too long before he held up those stages."

"Yeah, I'll admit to that. I told you he was trying real hard to talk me into joining up with him, and I told him no."

"Can you prove that?"

"That I told him no? Now, how would I go about proving that? It would be my word against his…if you could find him."

"No. I don't care what you told him. What I want to know is if you joined him on those stage robberies."

"No, I didn't join him. And how would I go about proving I wasn't there, except to say that I turned right around and left Jamestown and come back here. The only one who might help me is that ferryman in Grayson, or that feller in that little eating place. I think I might've talked to them both the next day…but I couldn't tell you what day that was, seeing as I don't know myself. And I don't even know what day of the month it was when I ett breakfast in Jamestown with them Mexicans when Rufus Ingram butted in."

"Fair enough. I'll check your story out, but I still don't want you going very far until I get some answers."

"What about my cattle?" Chris almost yelled. "Don't they count for anything?"

"Yes, they happen to count for a lot. I've talked to that woman and I know what you paid her for that beef. And I also know that they should be arriving at your place sometime tomorrow, so I'd advise you to get out there real soon. But I *am* saying that I don't want you going anyplace else, except your place and here, until I get some answers."

"What about Sorenson and that feller named Bill? I told you that I saw them with Ingram that day on the trail."

"You let me worry about them." He paused at the door to point a finger in Chris' face. "I'm warning you, Baker, you keep away from them. I know you've got a score to settle, and I can't say as I blame you. But if you go confronting them, one of you is going to wind up killing someone, and Dick Purvis will lock up whoever is left, and hang them. And if he doesn't, I will."

******

Paco, the cowboy called Tex, and a half dozen vaqueros arrived with a hundred head of some of the best breeding stock Chris had ever seen about noon Thursday. The Yokuts went into an instant celebration, shouting and dancing, while a few mounted ponies bareback and helped the *vaqueros* herd the cattle across the creek. Paco and Tex slid off their horses and ambled to where Chris was lounging in the shade on the porch, beating the dust off their britches with their sombreros, with grins plastered on their faces.

"How do they look?" Tex drawled as Chris watched the animals splash around in the pond.

"Just about the prettiest scene I've ever seen."

"Yep. Ain't nothing any prettier, except maybe a new-born mustang colt."

"Ya got me there," Chris said. "I'd almost take that over most humans any day."

"Well now, I take that back," Tex said as he paused from rolling a cigarette, "my Rosa's mighty purdy, and there wasn't nothing purdier than Martha when she was born."

"Martha's your daughter?"

"Yep, one and the same." He struck a match on the sole of his boot and lit his smoke.

Paco stepped off the porch as a team of oxen pulling a Mexican cart topped the hill, it's wooden wheels squealing as if they were in pain. Paco motioned the driver toward a vacant spot in the middle of the yard, then ran back toward the creek as a second cart came into view, leading a couple of goats tied in the back. He guided that one nearer the creek.

"What's all this? I didn't buy any goats."

"No, but they like eating the critters. And Raul there, driving that contraption, is one hell of a cook. He plans on roasting up them critters and a dozen or so chickens he's got in crates. I suspect that if you'd count them out, you'd find a couple of extra beeves amongst yours that's gonna get roasted along with them goats."

"Sounds mighty good. But what for?"

"To celebrate the end of this here drive." Tex grinned and slapped Chris on the back. "Don't take much to get these folks to celebrating, and this is more'n reason enough. From what I hear, there's gonna be a bunch more riding in before the night's over, and don't expect them to be leaving anytime soon."

Chris soon discovered Tex was right. The place was crawling with Mexicans and Indians before the sun had completely dropped behind the Diablo Range. Quite a few had brought instruments and were busy making some of the finest music Chris could remember hearing, when a buckboard loaded with tents, kegs of wine and brandy pulled into the yard. There were enough bonfires and torches blazing to keep the place lit when darkness finally set in. Raul had both goats, a dozen chickens, and a steer roasting over two fires, while several women cooked tortillas and beans. Chris, remembering his experience at *Doña* Kilkenney's rancho, thought some of the concoctions looked hot enough to blow the top of his head off. He guided one of the women to where the kitchen was, and was promptly run out of his own house by a bunch of jabbering women. They were preparing a real fiesta, and from what he remembered from the last one he had attended, it might last a day or two.

Things really started jumping when *Doña* Kilkenney arrived with her husband and a bunch of children in another wagon. Her husband admitted he had resigned himself to the fact that he wouldn't be able to keep her from celebrating with her people, and he thought the wagon would be better than allowing her to ride a horse. Chris said he wasn't any doctor, but after seeing the way she handled the black stallion that day on their ranch, he didn't figure there was anything she couldn't do, once she set her mind to doing it, and it didn't matter how pregnant she was. He laughed heartily and toasted Chris with a glass of brandy. His wife joined them where they were perched on the edge of the porch, holding little Olga's hand.

"I hope you don't mind the way we took over your place, *Señor*. My people have had so much sorrow, I thought it was important for them to celebrate."

"No, I don't mind. It wasn't something I expected, but I think it's downright friendly."

"*Gracias*. Now, this young lady wants to know where that young man is? She has grown rather fond of him."

"William? I reckon he's back in Hills Ferry with his ma. He ain't here right now."

"Oh? That is too bad." She turned to say something to the little girl in Spanish. The girl looked crushed and jabbered something back. Chris guessed he'd never understand to his dying day, how anyone could talk as fast as these folks did and still understand each other.

"She wants to know if there is any chance of him coming before she has to leave?"

"Not likely, Ma'am. You see, that boy's daddy just died. And then there's some other things that happened. Let's just say, his ma ain't likely to be talking to no one, and especially not going to parties for awhile."

Chris knew the girl didn't like hearing the news by the look on her face, but she cheered a little when a few of Johnny's cousins got her involved in a game of hoop-rolling. Chris sat enjoying the music and watching the dancing until the wee hours of the morning. He found he was right about the stuff the women had cooked inside the large pots. It was tasty enough, but he thought it was hot enough to fire a cannon with.

******

Late the following morning Chris was busy mucking out Bruiser's stall, when Tex said another wagon was coming. Only it turned out not to be a wagon. It happened to be Chris' buggy, and it was carrying the Gibsons, with Mrs. Shafer and her children. They had Tom Cunningham following close by on his horse.

"Now, don't that beat all you've ever seen?" Chris said, wiping his face with his hanky. "Coming all the way out here just to give me grief."

"Why's that? From the way you and that boy was talking back at Mrs. Kilkenny's place, I thought you and his ma might be kind of sweet on each other," Tex said with a snigger.

"Not likely. She's probably come all the way out here to watch the sheriff arrest me."

Chapter 21

Some of those standing near the corral heard Chris' remark about the sheriff arresting him, and a huge crowd had gathered by the time the buggy came to a stop. Chris stepped forward to brace Tom Cunningham, knowing there wasn't a thing he could do if the man had really come to arrest him, especially since he wasn't wearing a gun. Besides, shooting a lawman wasn't the smartest thing a man could do, regardless of the reason.

"Howdy, Tom. What brings you way out here? Got some bad news?"

"No, Chris. I've actually got good news for you," he said, sliding off the horse, stiff-like.

Reverend Gibson climbed out of the buggy and began helping the women out, as a pint-sized blur dashed passed Chris to latch onto William. She was jabbering a mile a minute in Spanish, and only stopped long enough to give him a quick kiss on the cheek, before dragging him toward the other children playing roll the hoop. Mrs. Shafer stared at Chris open-mouthed, as everyone burst into laughter.

"What can I tell you? He's got himself an admirer," Chris said with a shrug. He had no more than gotten the words out when Mrs. Kilkenney squeezed through the crowd to take both women by the arms.

"Please come with me *Señoras*," she said with a smile. "If you are waiting on these men to act like gentlemen and take you to the comfort of the *casa*, I'm afraid you will be waiting in the sun for a long time."

She led them toward the house as if she owned the place, causing Chris to glance toward Tex, who simply shrugged. Chris didn't say anything, because she was relieving him of having to entertain Mrs. Shafer, and since he wasn't quite willing to forgive her for acting the fool and believing those lies, he was happy to let the doctor's wife have at it. He eyed the sheriff and gave a quick motion with his head before starting after the women toward the house.

"Might as well come along, Tom. They got themselves a real Mexican hoe-down going on over yonder. And you'll find yourself some mighty good eating vittles to go along with it."

"Don't mind if I do."

Chris waited until the sheriff had stuffed himself with at least one plateful and drunk a mug of wine before pulling up a box to where he was sitting on the porch.

"Alright, what's this good news you brung me?" he said, as one of the girls handed him another plate of goat meat and chili. Mrs. Shafer came through the door with a plate and paused a few feet away to listen.

"Well, your story checks out. Every word of it."

"Never thought it wouldn't. Too bad you had to go to all that trouble."

"No trouble as far as I'm concerned," he said over a mouthful of tortilla. "I only wish everyone I checked on was as clean as you are."

"Then you'd never find the crooks you were looking for," Chris said. Cunningham paused his chewing to stare a long minute before chuckling.

"You got me there. I still haven't figured out what your friends in town are up to. No one can place them at the holdups with Rufus Ingram, so I can't arrest them for that, but they're dirty just the same. They'll make a mistake sooner or later, and either me or Purvis will be there when they do."

"Maybe. They might go to stirring up something that'll get them killed and save y'all the trouble."

Cunningham stopped chewing to point a fork at Chris. "Now, don't you go looking for trouble, or I'll have to lock you up for sure. And I'd hate like hell to have to hang you for ridding the town of two of it's worst citizens."

"I don't plan on hunting any trouble, Tom, but I do have to go into town once in awhile for supplies. You know as well as I do that I can't go sending Johnny Garcia and his folks by themselves, the way things are. And every time I've been in Hills Ferry lately, Frank Sorenson's braced me one way or another. I'm getting mighty tired of it."

"Well, if you two tangle, you'd best make sure there are plenty of witnesses. And make damned sure he's the one who starts it. That's all I've got to say." He took another bite and chewed angrily. Chris took a healthy swig of coffee before grinning.

"I don't think either one of us will have to worry about that. Besides, like I said, I'm a right peaceable man, Tom. And I ain't gonna be looking for no trouble anyway. Enjoy your meal, and stay as long as you want." He got up to leave when the lawman's voice stopped him.

"You got any idea how much money you really have, Chris?"

"No, I don't. Why?" Chris noticed those within hearing suddenly grew quiet to listen.

"Well, you know you still have an interest in that mining project, don't you?"

"Yeah, but seeing as I ain't nowhere near there, I haven't taken much notice."

"No, I don't guess you have," Cunningham said, and paused to sip his wine. "Seems they have been making regular deposits on your behalf. Your banker friend thought my inquiry, and the idea that someone would accuse you of robbing a stage, was downright humorous. He claims you're worth close to half a million."

Several on the porch caught their breath, while others stood quietly staring. Chris knew the bank manager or someone must have made a mistake, because there was no way he had that much money, especially after spending close to seven-thousand dollars on the ranch and cattle.

"Na," he said, shaking his head. "I know I had me a little bit, but not near that much. They got me mixed up with someone else."

"Nope, afraid not. Got the telegram right here. Read it for yourself," Cunningham said, pulling a folded sheet of paper from his pocket. "Seems you are a rich man, Chris. And somehow the word of your wealth, and where it came from, has gotten spread around town. I think you can credit Mrs. Shafer's son and that friend of yours at the livery for telling folks. But you're the talk of the town. Don't be surprised if someone isn't trying to sell you something at every turn in the road."

"If you had explained this to everyone from the beginning, none of this trouble would have happened," Mrs. Shafer said softly.

"Maybe. But like I tried telling you, and anyone else who would listen, I don't think it is anyone's business how much money anyone has. Besides, seeing as the Bakers never had any, money's never meant that much to me. Until I got ready to buy this here place, and the cattle, I just didn't think about it. Well, I did buy the buggy," he said, and paused to take another sip of coffee, "but that was because it reminded me of my ma. And what little I spent on you and the boy was needed and didn't amount to a whole lot."

"Not a whole lot? I beg to differ with you Mr. Baker. You supported us for almost three months. I realize it was mostly my fault. I should have written my parents and moved into town and looked for employment long ago. No wonder people began getting the wrong idea about our relationship. I am terribly sorry."

"Well, what people in town choose to think, or not think, ain't the issue as far as I'm concerned. They're gonna believe what they want. It was you and the boy thinking I was a thief that done me in. I would've thought you'd be different from all the rest, but, I guess you ain't. That's what

I get for trusting a Yankee," Chris said. He stomped off the porch, past those that were listening and toward the creek.

******

"Okay, tell me then. Why are you treating her this way?" Johnny Garcia grabbed Chris' arm as he tried turning away.

"Remember who you're working for, boy," Chris warned, and jerked his arm from the boy's grip.

"I am remembering. And I don't know what's happened to that man. He seems to have disappeared. Where is he, Chris? What's happened to you?"

"Nothing you'd understand."

"Try me."

"What business is it of yours? Why are you so interested in how I treat Mrs. Shafer, or any other woman, for that matter?"

"I'm interested because something is eating you inside, and it's killing everything that's important to you."

"Such as?"

"Such as you and that woman." Johnny pointed toward the house. Chris couldn't help but see the crowd on the porch staring back, and was tempted to bust Johnny in the chops and leave. But he knew the boy was only trying to help, and busting folks he liked wasn't the way he normally settled things.

"There never was anything between us, except for my trying to help her when her husband ran off. And now that she's asked her parents for help and moved to Hills Ferry, I don't reckon she's my problem anymore. So, I don't have to worry about her, do I? Fact is, I don't even have to think about her, if I don't really want to. See?" Chris said, staring at him real hard. "I ain't even thinking about her right now. I cleared her out of my head for good."

"Okay," Johnny said with a laugh. "Let me see you go to her and tell her that in front of all those people. Go ahead." He pointed.

"You want me to embarrass her in front of all those people?"

"Sure. You've already embarrassed her in front of them once, so it shouldn't make much difference. Besides, you said she doesn't mean anything to you."

"I can't do that, Johnny," Chris said, backing away. "That's plumb mean."

"Why should you care? That is, unless she does mean something to you. In which case, you owe her an explanation."

"Smart-alec Indian," Chris said with a scowl. The Indian laughed and continued pointing toward the porch. "It's gonna be one long month in July before you get yourself a raise," Chris added before turning away.

He didn't want to admit it, but he knew the boy was right. He did owe Mrs. Shafer something, regardless of how wrong she'd been. But knowing didn't help the way he felt, and he found it was a long walk back to where the folks sat staring. What made things worse was, they kept right on staring as he made the journey from the creek to the porch. Just to get back at them, Chris took his sweet time pouring a cup of coffee and finding the perfect spot to perch himself on the porch railing. Then, after taking a long swig of the brew, he stared back at Mrs. Shafer.

"Okay," he said after a minute, "I offer my apologies to everyone here, especially to you, Ma'am. I reckon I've been acting the fool, and deserved folks thinking the way they've been. Besides, I've never cottoned to anyone who went around holding grudges, but I reckon I've been doing just that where you're concerned. You can't help it none, being born a danged Yankee."

Mrs. Shafer's mouth dropped open as Chris stood and winked at Mrs. Kilkenney. Everyone but Mrs. Shafer burst out laughing, and a couple of the musicians struck up a happy tune. Chris grabbed Olga's hand and half-drug the little girl into the yard and proceeded to dance up a jig. They were about half done, when Mrs. Shafer cut in.

"Danged Yankee, am I?"

"Yes'm, I reckon you are."

"Well, Mr. Baker, let's see if a danged Southerner can keep up with this Yankee." She hiked the hem of her skirt and began stomping out one of the best Irish jigs Chris had seen. The musicians saw what was happening, and took into playing right along with her. Chris hated to admit it, but he was hard pressed keeping up with her, and his ma had claimed him to be the best barn dancer anywhere in Georgia. He knew his mother's assumption was up for debate, but figured Mrs. Shafer to be a fine dancer, and right pretty to boot. The way she grinned as she danced caused Chris to stumble over his own feet a time or two, and he was glad when the music stopped.

Their dancing caused the mood to lighten considerably, and Chris had almost forgotten the anger he had felt on the porch, until he'd gone inside to fetch another tin of coffee. He was busy rummaging through one of the cupboards when he heard a bunch of stomping and foot-scraping in the living room. He turned to see Mrs. Shafer, Reverend and Mrs. Gibson, Tom and Mrs. Kilkenney staring at him.

"Y'all got something on yer mind?"

"Yes," Mrs. Shafer said. "Everyone would like to know your story. It might help us understand."

"I see." Chris bounced the can of coffee several times in his hand before passing it off to one of the women who'd taken over his kitchen. "Okie-dokie, if that's the way it's got to be. Come on inside and close the door. The rest will just have to wait and hear it from y'all."

Mrs. Kilkenney promptly shooed the women in the kitchen outside while jabbering a mile a minute in Spanish. Then, after checking the bedrooms, she gave the all clear signal and waited until everyone was seated. She had started to bolt the door, when one of the women handed her a steaming mug of coffee, and said it was for Chris. He accepted the cup and waited until she had seated herself before clearing his throat.

"Like I said once before, the Bakers left Tennessee and settled in Georgia looking for a better life. We didn't have a lot as some folks count things, but we done alright. Pa, while he lived, and us boys, farmed that little patch of ground we owned and did ourselves right proud. We even did a little sharecropping for some neighbors. We also hunted, did some hauling, woodcutting...most anything we could to bring the coon home.

"One of the neighbor families we sharecropped with was considered rich folks, and had them a pretty young daughter named Amy. Amy Butler had the blackest hair and eyes you ever saw, and cutest little turned-up nose and smile. She was downright pretty, and just about as perfect as the Good Lord could've made her. Well, me and Amy taken a shine to each other, but her pa, he didn't think none too highly of the idee. He said I was a no-account sharecropper, and his daughter could do a whole lot better. I told him I agreed. Amy could've had most any man she wanted. But seeing as how we really loved each other, and I had already joined up to fight in the war, I was hoping he'd at least give me the chance to prove myself when I come back.

"Well, he agreed to my calling on her until I went off to war. Then, we continued writing each other for awhile. There were some folks who claimed I'd done some mighty great things, moving up in the ranks the way I'd done. In one of her last letters, Amy said her pa was right proud of me. But if the truth were known, it was mostly because there were so many boys dying on both sides that caused fellers like me to get their ranking. Before I knowed what was happening, here I was, a full-blown captain with a passel of men under me. And the longer the war went, it became apparent to me who was gonna win, not because them fellers on the north side were better at fighting than we were -- I don't really think they could fight as well, seeing as most of us southern boys were corn-fed, coon-huntin' scrapers, who'd been shooting since we were knee-high to a grasshopper -- But them that was on the north had a steady supply of guns, ammunition, food and medical supplies, while us boys were cold and hungry most of the time. And right near the end, we didn't even have enough powder to put up a decent scrap against a pack of hound dogs.

"It was at one of them battles when fellers like Reb started calling me *Nails Baker*, 'cause they figured I was tough as nails. The truth was, we was penned down without much to fight with, and them Yanks just kept a-coming. I got tired of seeing fellers I'd known most of my life getting all shot to hell. And when one of them Yanks put a ball into a young boy of only thirteen years old, who wasn't doing nothing but holding our flag, something inside me snapped. I jumped over the barricade and charged them Yankees, yelling and firing off my pistol like a wounded Comanche. Well, when them reb soldiers under my command saw me, they come a charging right on my heels. What we done surprised them Yanks so much, they taken tail and run like scare't rabbits. I remember picking up a gun one of the Yanks dropped and giving one of them a dose of their own lead. I reckon the boys with me were doing much the same thing, 'cause, like I said, we didn't have much to fight with. Well, they kinda figured I was some sort of hero and gave me a medal. Truth was, I didn't know much of what I was doing, and should've gotten myself kilt, like a lot of the boys did. But for some reason, none of them Yanks shot close enough to even scratch me. Well, later on, them Yanks regrouped and kept right on coming until there wasn't enough of us to do nothing but surrender.

"After the war, I finally came home and found there wasn't any home to come home to. Ma and Pa both were dead. Sherman had somehow seen to it his march included our little patch of ground and burnt everything, including the house, to the ground. Both my brothers had been killed during the war. Viola, my sister, had gotten herself married off to some feller and had moved to Texas. Couldn't say as I blamed her none. Then I went to see Amy." Chris stopped and took another sip of coffee before continuing.

"Well, it seems some of them yellow-legs who were with Sherman had abused her something fierce. Then they burnt the Butler place to the ground like they'd done everything else. But the way they'd done Amy caused her to completely lose her mind. Her pa said she just sat there, in the shade of that old willow, and pined away. They couldn't get her to eat or drink nothing a'tall. She was all dead inside, and sat staring at nothing, until her body just quit breathing.

"Well, I figured there wasn't no need of me hanging around, so I borrowed Bruiser from a drunken Yankee officer and headed west. I didn't have me no plan. I just pointed that horse and let him wander."

"Is that how you wound up in Colorado?" Tom Cunningham asked.

"I reckon."

"How'd you find all that gold?"

"I didn't. That old trapper did. Like I said, I'd developed a habit of letting Bruiser go pretty much where he wanted. That day, he'd taken an old trail that was all grown over and hadn't been traveled much. Along sunset, we come into a clearing with this little two-room cabin. Well, I hollered some, and pounded on the door, but no one answered a word. So, I kicked the door open, and there he sat, all dried out and deader'n bleached bones. Been dead most of a year from what I seen.

"Well, I gave the old feller a proper burial and started noising around inside that cabin. He had enough skins and furs in that back room to make most fellers rich. But down under all them skins, was sack after sack of gold. Seems he'd run across some sort of bonanza whilst trapping. He must've gotten greedy and fiddled around, getting himself snowed in for the winter. Then, seeing as you can't eat gold, why he just up and starved to death.

"I packed what little I could on ol' Bruiser, along with what personal items the feller had, and headed into Denver. I found me a fancy lawyer who looked like he had no cause to steal from the likes of me, and told him what I run into. He did some checking, and it seems that old trapper didn't have a living relative anywheres to be found. So, the lawyer, he tells me to file a claim on that cabin and the surrounding land, which I done. Then, I taken me a bunch of pack mules and hauled all them furs and gold back to Denver. In the meantime, seeing as how neither one of us knew much about mining, this lawyer had located a large mining firm interested in our claim. Bottom line is, we both got more money than any man deserves, and I was free to go and do as much as I pleased, which is what I done. I pointed Bruiser south and wound up here."

"You once told me that *Nails Baker* was a man who had made a name for himself as a gunfighter and killer, Mr. Baker," Mrs. Shafter said. "Are you a gunfighter who has killed people?" The way she kept her eyes glued on Chris made him uncomfortable.

"I suppose some might be calling me that. Amy's pa was with me when we run into that Yankee who had Bruiser. Now, here's something ya gotta understand. Bruiser was Amy's horse, and I've known that critter from the time he was born. Her pa said he remembered seeing that feller the night they raided and burnt their place to the ground, and he said he was for sure that he was one of them that abused Amy. He didn't deny it none when I braced him either. He was still laughing when I bored him right through the gizzard. Then a couple more blue-coats come running when they heard the shots, so I bored them too. That's when I jumped on Bruiser and headed west. And I'll admit to killing a couple more of them Yankees before getting out of town." He paused to stare at Tom Cunningham a long minute before placing the empty cup on the floor.

"Now, if you want to arrest me for boring them skunks that killed and abused my Amy, and for liberating a good horse from a murdering Yankee, go right ahead. I won't fight you none, 'cause I done it."

"I'm not concerned about what might have happened in Georgia after the war. There's probably a hell of a lot worse than what you told me going on right this minute."

"The day you arrived at our door, I took you for a saddle tramp, Mr. Baker. And I believe everyone who's met you since came to the same conclusion. Why...did you...allow us to believe that?" Mrs. Shafer shook her head at him.

"Well, I reckon that's what I was, Ma'am. The fact I had a little money didn't change what I was, or what I had been living like. I'd just spent the most of two weeks coming from Los Angeles getting to your front door. In my book, that makes me a saddle tramp." Chris got up and stared out the window.

"Now, y'all know about me. I'm a no-account saddle tramp that's fresh out of the war, who has himself quite a bit of money. But I ain't never took nothing that didn't belong to me, (except for that horse), and I never killed no one who didn't need killing. For the most part, I'm God-fearing, and right peaceable. And the only thing I want right now is just to be left alone and raise beef critters."

Chris waited until they'd cleared the living room, before slipping out the back and saddling Bruiser. He followed the creek away from the house, before heading toward Poverty Flat. He knew there wasn't anything there, except the ornery beef critters, lizards, and snakes. But telling his story had resurrected a lot of things he didn't feel like remembering. Lizards, snakes and beef critters seem better than having to face Mrs. Shafer any time soon. He had discovered what had been bothering him while telling his story. He saw it when she smiled and thanked him before following the rest out onto the porch. Mary Ellen Shafer had Amy Butler's smile.

Chapter 22

It was past midnight when Chris turned Bruiser loose inside the corral. By the look of things, his leaving had caused the party to break up, and the yard was nearly empty. But he'd had a wagonload of thinking to do, and had drifted around among the grazing cattle at Poverty Flat, mulling things over long after the sun had dropped behind the Diablos. Right now he was tired, and plopped on the edge of his bed to pull his boots off. Then, stripping down to his long johns, he rolled over and dozed off on top of his blankets. He woke just after sunup to the smell of fresh-brewed coffee and bacon.

"It's about time you crawled out of bed."

Chris stared, speechless. He had taken it for granted that her and the boy had gone, same as everyone else.

"Sit down and drink your coffee," she said with a nod, as she cracked several eggs into the pan. "How do you like your eggs? Hard or over-easy?"

"Pardon?" Chris said, taking a sip of the brew. It was a little weaker than he was used to, but still tasty. A mongrel pup that belonged to one of the Indians trotted over to lay by his chair.

"I said, how do you want your eggs cooked." She looked at him slantwise with a grin.

"Oh, it don't make me no never mind. Just any old way."

"Okay, you'll get them medium-well," she said, sliding a plateful of bacon and hot biscuits in front of him.

"But you might get them raw next time, if you don't learn to speak up."

"Where's the boy?" Chris said, biting into a piece of bacon.

"William's already had his breakfast, and left with Johnny to check on the cattle. Johnny's father said a mountain lion killed one of them last night." She poured herself a cup and stared at Chris from where she stood at the stove.

"Figures. How come you're still here? Ain't you afraid folks back in town are gonna talk?"

"They are already talking, Mr. Baker. How much more damage do you think they can do? Besides, Reverend Gibson said he would send your friend from the livery stable tomorrow with the buggy for William and me. In the meantime, you and I have business to discuss."

"Ma'am?" He took a bite of biscuit as she slid the eggs onto his plate. She returned the pan to the stove and retrieved her cup, then sat across from him at the table.

"Poverty Flat. You are grazing cattle on my land, if I'm not mistaken."

"Yes, Ma'am. Is that a problem?"

"No, but seeing as how it is my land, don't you think I should receive some sort of compensation?"

"Yes, Ma'am. I just took it for granted that you and the boy wanted to go into the ranching business, same as me. And seeing as he's been working for me, I'd figured on helping y'all out by giving the loan of some cattle to get yourselves started."

"That's very thoughtful of you, Mr. Baker. And how do you suppose we are going to live? As you have noted yourself, that little shack wasn't really meant to live in for very long, let alone raise a family there."

"Well, I'd reckoned on having the Indians build y'all a right-nice place to stay in. And I've been asking around some, and Simon says he knows of a feller who'll dig y'all a nice deep well, so you'll have all the fresh water you need.

Poverty Flat

And the boy can keep right on working and earning wages so you can buy things you might be needing. I figured it might be a little hard at first, but between me and the Indians, we can help you build a right nice place on Poverty Flat."

"Oh," she said with a nod. "I guess you've been doing yourself a lot of *figuring*, haven't you, Mr. Baker?"

He knew he'd somehow gotten himself into more trouble, but for all the cotton in Georgia, couldn't recollect how. Chris paused chewing and swallowed a mouthful of egg as she kept talking.

"What about me, Mr. Baker? Shouldn't I have been consulted while you were doing all your *figuring*? Especially since you were going to build us a house? Weren't you even going to ask my opinion as to what kind of house? How many rooms? And...and...what type of curtains to hang in the window, or type of storage in the kitchen? Those things are important to a woman, Mr. Baker. And just where were you *figuring* on building this *tolerable* house for us to live in? Poverty Flat is a rather large piece of land. And besides all that, what if I didn't choose to live there? All your work and figuring would have been for nothing, wouldn't it, Mr. Baker?"

The longer she talked, the redder she got in the face, until she jumped up from the table and stormed out the door. Chris sat quietly staring at the door she'd banged shut, still wondering what he had done that'd gotten her so riled. Then he heard the sound of a girl giggling, and turned to see Cola`we watching through the open window.

"You don't understand women very well, do you *señor*?"

"No, I don't guess I do. At least not that Yankee. What'd I do that caused her to pitch such a fit?"

"That's something you should ask her *señor*. Women like to be asked such things. You should go tell her you're sorry for leaving her out of your plans and ask her forgiveness."

"I always thought women liked being taken care of."

"They do." She cocked her head slantwise and giggled. "But they also like to feel they are in control...at least of their own house. You made a big mistake. And now she is very angry with you." She disappeared and Chris could hear her giggling as she ran toward the creek.

"Danged women anyways," he growled, whacking at his eggs with the fork. He hadn't known a female that didn't cause the most peace-loving type of man some sort of trouble. He also remembered reading in the Bible where it was Eve, the first woman ever created, that ate the apple and caused her husband Adam to go sinning. If he recollected right, she had eaten the apple because she started listening to a snake in the grass instead of her husband and the good Lord Himself. It was enough to make a man wonder if God hadn't made a mistake creating females in the first place.

Chris didn't suppose it mattered any, except he had somehow gotten himself tied up with this one just by trying to be nice. And she was somehow more complicated than most females he'd known. Nothing like his own ma, for instance. You knew exactly what was on that woman's mind every second, because she'd let you know. Besides, she was kind of like Cola`we, in that her wants and needs were simple-like. Things a man could handle right easy. As long as the field was plowed, animals taken care of, and she had vittles she could whip together to make a meal, ma was happy enough. Other than that, the only thing she wanted most was her family by her side. But this Yankee was the worst woman he'd ever seen. He couldn't figure from one second to the next what was in her pea-brain. Chris shoved the eggs away and stomped into the bedroom to sit on the edge of the bed and pull his boots on.

"One day she's ready to scratch your eyes out because you're trying to get her out of that flea-bitten shack, and into some nice hotel room or house in town." He was talking out loud to the dog who had followed him into the bedroom. "Then, when you decide to build her a nice place to live in, right where she claims to want to live, why she throws it in your face like you'd somehow insulted her."

He paused at the table long enough to gulp down the rest of his coffee, and give the eggs to the dog. Then, jamming his hat down on his head, Chris stomped out the door. He spied her perched on a log, near where Johnny's folks had dammed the creek, rocking Edith in her arms. The scene caused him to wonder where the girl had been during their ruckus. Johnny and William rode in as Chris walked a beeline to where she was sitting.

"Ma'am, it 'pears to me that I've somehow offended you, although for the life of me, I can't figure out why."

"You can't, Mr. Baker?"

"No, Ma'am."

"Well, for one thing, you should have consulted me first, when considering the welfare of me and my children."

"Yes, Ma'am, I suppose you're right. But I was only trying to do something nice."

"Don't you think I know that? You...you've done nothing but be kind and compassionate toward us since the day we met you, and we will be forever in your debt for as long as we live."

"I don't understand. What's the problem then?" Chris said, loud enough to make Edith jerk.

"The problem is," she said standing to glare at him, "you've constantly, since the day we met, been making plans and decisions for me and my children. You've been telling me where I have to live, where to go, where and what to eat, you've even taken it upon yourself to buy the clothes I wear."

"Now, wait a minute. You were the one who decided we needed to eat at that fancy place in San Francisco that tried serving us bugs and creepy things to eat. And I thought you looked right pretty in those dresses I got you."

"Yes, I did choose to dine in that French restaurant, and they served escargot, not *bugs and creepy things*."

"Still looked like something ma used to stomp on inside her garden. But I think the dresses were right pretty."

"Oh, they are, Mr. Baker," she said, glancing at the squirming baby and back again. "But I would have liked being asked my opinion instead of you handing me a boxful of clothing and saying *here, put 'em on*."

"Well, pardon my thick-headedness."

"We're not married, Mr. Baker. And I'm not your paramour, regardless of what the town might think."

"I reckon you're not, whatever that's supposed to mean."

"Lover," she snapped.

"You've got that right, lady," he said and stomped toward the corral. William caught up with Chris as he snagged Bruiser's bridle from the peg on the side of the shed.

"Johnny and me found where that mountain lion that's killing cattle is holed up," he said, as Chris opened the gate.

"Well, you've got a gun. Go kill it," he snapped. The boy was taken aback, and Chris knew he didn't deserve to be barked at, but he wasn't feeling too friendly at the moment.

He tossed the saddle on Bruiser's back and led him to the creek to drink his fill while topping off his canteen.

"Johnny says he should have a bigger gun than the Remington to go after a lion."

"Well, here," Chris said, pulling the Winchester and giving it a toss. "Careful, it's loaded." He climbed on Bruiser and glared down at him.

"It holds seven shots. But it should only take one, two at the most, to kill that cat." He spurred the horse toward Poverty Flat without any real plan as to what he might be doing or when he was coming back.

******

Poverty Flat

He found himself on the west end of Poverty Flat about mid-afternoon where the grassland rolled up easily to meet the rocks and slope at the foot of the Diablo range. He'd also found the carcass of the half-eaten steer, but since he had foolhardily tossed William the Winchester, there wasn't any way Chris would consider cougar-hunting with a pistol. Besides, he figured the Yokut would make short order of the cat as soon as he and the boy had rested some.

Chris had just gotten down to study some fresh tracks made by two shod horses when the bullet knocked him flat. Bruiser neighed at the sound of the gunshot, but being the old warhorse he was, he stood, pawing the ground, and waiting orders. Chris crawled to the horse, wrapped his arm through the stirrup and yelled. He had joked from time to time about a horse knowing its master better than a woman, but the way Bruiser acted caused him to believe his jesting might be true. The horse trotted toward the rocks, dragging and shielding him from whoever was doing the shooting. Chris waited until they were a few feet from a good outcropping before turning him loose with a swat on the rump. Then, he half ran and half drug himself to safety and took stock of his wound.

Whoever it was had plugged him pretty good, high in the back, just left of the spine. The wound felt like someone had jammed a hot branding iron halfway through his body, and from the look of things, he was losing a good amount of blood. It wasn't hard to figure who it was that wanted him dead. Outside of Frank Sorenson, the only other person he figured he might've angered since arriving, was Mrs. Shafer. And while he seemed to have the knack for riling her nearly every day, Chris had never took her to do any back-shooting. Besides, after seeing her shoot, he reckoned she was good enough to have opened the top of his head with one shot. He peered over the rocks he was hiding behind and could see them coming, Frank and his buddy Billy, riding slow, trying to figure out where he'd gone.

"Good God," Chris said with a groan. "What a way to end up Christian Baker, hiding behind a patch of rocks, on a hunk of land called Poverty Flat, with a hole in your back that's bleeding something fierce. What's worse, you ain't got a horse, no canteen or rifle, and two hydrophobied skunks fixin' to kill you. Well, why not?" He pulled the .44 from it's holster and cocked the hammer. "All I was hoping was to have a pleasant breakfast and spend a quiet day enjoying my cattle. But, dying might be a good way to end it after all."

Chapter 23

Chris waited until he figured they were about as close as he wanted, then cut loose with a couple of rounds. The only thing he succeeded in doing was killing Frank's horse, when he had been aiming at Frank. He leaned against the rock, guessing the hole in his back was causing more trouble than he wanted to admit. If he'd been a cussing man, he might have done some at the sight of the horse falling, and Frank running for cover. They sent a few rounds his way, but nothing came close enough to cause Frank any alarm. Frank jumped on the other horse behind Billy, and Chris fired a couple more shots as they galloped away.

He waited until he was fairly certain they weren't coming back before relaxing and reloading the gun. The sun was warm, and he was having trouble focusing by the time he had finished loading and had tucked the Colt back into its holster. Chris remembered closing his eyes to rest, followed by the sound of people talking inside a hollow log.

******

"Ma!" Chris jumped at William's shrill voice. "Ma!" the boy hollered again and ran toward the bedroom door. "He's awake, Ma."

Chris didn't know if he was really awake or dreaming, because he was having trouble focusing on exactly where he was. Nothing seemed to be in the right place, and there were different colored curtains hanging over the window. Fact was, he couldn't even remember having curtains in his bedroom, because he didn't see any need of having to buy curtains when a saddle blanket worked just as good. Besides not being able to focus, his throat was dryer than a year-old corncob that'd been left in the sun, and his entire body felt like he'd been run over by a herd of buffalo. Chris had just remembered being shot, when Mrs. Shafer came into the room, followed by Velma Gibson.

"So he is," Mrs. Shafer said with a smile.

"How are you feeling, Mr. Baker?" Velma asked, feeling his brow with a cool hand.

His answer sounded more like a croak than anything, and Mrs. Shafer propped his head in her left hand as she let him drink from a glass of water.

"God bless you," he said falling back to the pillow. "Where am I?"

"You are in our spare bedroom, Mr. Baker," Velma said. "You were gunshot, you know."

"I reckon I knowed that, Ma'am. I just don't remember coming here. In fact, all I remember is getting myself shot, firing back and killing a horse, then reloading as I watched them back-shooting skunks ride away. How'd I get here anyway?"

"Mrs. Shafer and her son brought you here in the buggy to be closer to the doctor."

"That right? I'm much obliged, Ma'am," he said, looking at Mrs. Shafer.

"That is quite alright, Mr. Baker. Think nothing of it. Besides, it was William and Johnny Garcia that actually rescued you. They had gone looking for that mountain lion as you had ordered, when they heard the shots and saw the two men fleeing on one horse. Johnny was able to follow your tracks to where you were lying in the rocks. Somehow, they managed to get you onto your horse and back to the house. We were able to stop the bleeding before moving you into town." She paused to stare intently before continuing.

"Doctor Hall removed the bullet and said you came close to dying."

"That ain't surprising. Rifle slugs have a tendency to do that sort of thing."

"Oh, you...!" She tied her mouth into a tiny bow and glared. "Do you have to make light of everything?" She then whirled with a swish of her skirts and stormed out of the room.

"Now, what'd I do?" Chris croaked as Velma giggled.

"She's been so worried about you. We all have. But it's been Mrs. Shafer who has taken it upon herself to be your nurse. She has spent countless hours these past few days here at your bedside, looking out after you."

Chris decided there wasn't much one could say about that. So, he made up his mind to thank her next time she came into the room. Besides, he was feeling kind of woosey, and decided to close his eyes for just a minute. It was dark outside when he opened them, and then Tom Cunningham was the next one Velma ushered into the room. There was a handsome man with a black moustache with him.

"Howdy, Chris," Tom said with a nod. "This here's Dick Purvis, sheriff around these parts.

"Howdy," Chris returned the greeting.

"Well, doc says you're gonna make it," Dick Purvis said.

"I reckon. But I don't know how he'd know, seeing as I ain't seen him yet."

"Well, he's seen you enough to know you're gonna live," Tom said with a chuckle. He pulled up a chair and stared for a minute as the smile left his face.

"Johnny and Mrs. Shafer's son are saying that it was Frank Sorenson and Bill Grant who tried to dry gulch you. That right?"

"I reckon you can take that to the bank and deposit it, if you've a mind to," Chris said with a nod.

"Well, Dick would like to do just that, and so would I. But Sorenson and Grant are saying it was someone else.

And when they tried to help you, you opened fire on them, killing one of their horses."

"You ain't swallowing that hogwash, are you Tom?"

"Not likely. But we need something more from you on them boys to arrest them," Dick said.

"Like what? I got a bullet in my back, and them fellers were out there on Poverty Flat. What more do you need than that?"

"Like a witness. Someone who saw them pull the trigger. Look," Dick said leaning close, "I know how you feel, and I ain't blaming you none. But if I arrested them now, and brought them to trial with what evidence I've got, they'd get off scott-free."

"I don't see how."

"Well, seeing as you were shot in the back, it's not likely you saw who pulled the trigger, did you?"

Chris shook his head.

"Didn't think so. And seeing as there were two of them, and only one bullet in your back, I wouldn't know which one to arrest. And seeing as they are saying they were only out hunting on Poverty Flat, like dozens of other folks around here, I can't charge them with breaking any law."

"Fact is," Tom said as he shifted in his chair, "Frank was claiming you ought to pay for killing his horse. Dick said if he insisted on making you pay, he was gonna hound him and throw his ornery hide in jail every other day for being a nuisance. There isn't anyone in Hills Ferry that doesn't believe they were the ones who shot you, but we need something more to go on."

The longer they talked, the more Chris knew they were right, and the yellow-livered, back-shooting skunks were going to get away with trying to dry gulch him.

"Well, I'm sorry, but I ain't got eyes in the back of my head, and I can't tell y'all more'n I already have. But I will tell you this, and it's the gospel truth. If they ever come after me again, I'm danged sure gonna fight back, and I ain't gonna be killing no innocent horses."

"I figured it might be coming to that. Just make sure if that time ever comes there's some witnesses around to verify you were only defending yourself," Dick said.

"And what if they try dry gulching me again like they did the other day?"

"Well, if that happens, either bury their carcasses and don't say nothing, or drag 'em back to your place and make it look like you were trying to defend your home."

"Better yet," Tom said and got up to take hold of the door handle and grin, "and you didn't hear this from me…if you're gonna kill them, make sure it's in the middle of town where no one can miss what happens. That way, Dick will have plenty of witnesses."

******

"Ma'am," Chris said, as he joined Mrs. Shafer's side on the front porch. It was two days later, and he was still feeling weak in body, but busting to get back out to the ranch and get things moving.

"The doctor says you should be staying in bed, Mr. Baker. You don't mind very well, do you?" She cocked her head to give him a crooked grin.

"Reckon not. It's a nice evening, ain't it?" he said, taking in a deep breath of fresh night air. "I was beginning to feel like I was suffocating inside the bedroom, even with the windows open."

"Yes, it certainly is a nice evening."

"Where's Edith and the boy?"

"Edith is asleep, and William went back to your ranch with Johnny Garcia and Mr. Ross from the livery."

"Reb? Why's he out there? Is there something wrong with one of the horses?"

"No," she giggled, "so don't go worrying yourself. Mr. Ross sold his business to one of the owners of the other stable. According to him, it seemed you needed another *good ol' southern boy* out at your place to see that things were being run right while you were laid up."

"Well," Chris said with a chuckle, "that's a mighty fine thing for him to do, and I'm mighty happy to be having his help. But I kind of figured that Johnny and William could have handled most anything that come along."

"Yes, I'm certain they can. But, seeing as William won't be working for you much longer, I'm sure you will find Mr. Ross's presence very helpful."

"William's not…say," Chris said, turning to frown at her, "you're still not upset about folks thinking he's been taken up with a thief and robber, are you?"

"No, Mr. Baker," she said laying a hand against his arm. "That argument has been laid to rest long ago. It's just that I received a wire from my parents for fare aboard a ship back to New York. Now, I'm just waiting for the wire to clear the bank, and to decide what I'm going to do with Poverty Flat, and then we will be leaving. The problem with Poverty Flat was one of the things I was trying to work out with you the day you got shot." She turned to stare full into his face. The news of her leaving, and staring at him with those eyes, did funny things to his insides.

"Do you want to purchase Poverty Flat, Mr. Baker?"

"I don't know. I ain't thought much about it, Mrs. Shafer."

"Well, I wish you would think about it over the next few days. I will be having to make a decision fairly soon." She smiled and went inside, leaving him feeling as though he had a bucket of Mexican jumping beans in the pit of his stomach.

It wasn't that he had any claim on her or the kids, he reasoned, because he didn't. And, although it seemed like they always wound up barking and snapping at each other most every time they talked, he hated to hear she was leaving. He was going to miss that boy something powerful-like, and kind of figured he had some sort of claim on that baby, seeing as he was the one who helped bring her into the world. The truth was, when he had finally shucked down to the cob, Chris was going to miss Mrs. Shafer something awful...even if she wasn't anything but a Yankee. She was a pretty Yankee, and about as nice a one as he'd ever run into. Besides, he reasoned, if the good Lord could forgive him for some of the things he'd done, he reckoned he should forgive her for being a Yankee.

The more he thought about her leaving, the more Chris knew he didn't want them to go. But he was hanged if he could figure out a way to keep her from going.

Chapter 24

"When I decided Irene was the woman for me, I went ahead and told her so, and she made me one happy man, God bless her soul."

"Huh?" Chris looked up from the nail he was trying to drive into the fence post. He was helping Reb and Johnny build an extension onto the corral, when Reb started talking nonsense.

"I said, when I decided I wanted to marry Irene, I went ahead and told her so, instead of moping around like some love-sick puppy."

"Well, first of all, I don't even know what yer talking about. I ain't seen as how Johnny's been moping around none," Chris growled, and promptly whacked his left thumb with the hammer. "Ow! Dang it," he yelled, dancing around.

"Ya don't, huh? Then why'd you smash yer thumb, instead of hitting the nail?" He paused to spit while Johnny doubled over laughing.

"Well, I'm sure glad you think my pain is funny. I hit my thumb because you distracted me from what I was doing."

"Not hardly," Reb grunted, and drove his nail flush with two whacks.

"Reb is right," Johnny said, as he hoisted another rail into place. "You have been moping around since you came back."

"Don't you think getting shot in the back might have something to do with that?" Chris said with a sneer.

Poverty Flat

"Hardly. I've seen the day when getting shot would only cause you to get madder than hell and fight all the harder. Besides, it'd take more'n that little bullet in yer back to cause you to act the way yer doing," Reb said. He paused to take a healthy bite off his plug of chew as he studied Chris. "Didn't you ever read where a man can go to hell just as easily for lying as he can for murder?"

"Well, can't say as I ever kilt no one who didn't deserve killing, or come at me shooting first. So, I don't think the good Lord's gonna be holding what killing I might've done against me. And what makes you think I'm lying about something when I don't even know what you're talking about?"

"There he goes again," Reb said, glancing at Johnny. The Yokut went into another fit that caused him to double over laughing. Chris backed away and glared until the boy had composed himself.

"I think what Reb is trying to say is, you don't really want Mrs. Shafer to take her children and return to New York because you are in love with her."

Chris knew the Indian had a way of cutting right to the bone with those words of his, and he didn't have any way of coming back at him.

"If I were you, instead of standing there and staring like an idgit, I'd pack my best clothes, ride into town and check into the hotel early. Then, I'd go to the barber and get all cleaned up and take a hot bath. After that, I'd go to Simon's store and buy a box of candy, and maybe pick some flowers, and go see her. Then I'd take her to some place nice and quiet, without the children, and tell her exactly how I felt. Then I'd take her into my arms and ask her to marry me, and, if she said yes, I'd kiss her." Johnny finished with a nod before driving a nail flush in three whacks.

"Well, seeing as you have a way with words, why don't you go do all them things for me?"

"Because, my friend," He placed a hand on Chris' shoulder and grinned, "she would be marrying me, instead of you. Now, you tell me honestly, would that solve your problem?"

He turned away and grabbed another rail, hoisting it into place. "Come on, Reb. You and I will have to finish this corral. Our friend has more important things to do."

"Well, the way he's standing there like a thunderstruck Yankee, I don't know if he's gonna go take care of business or not."

"It makes no difference if he does or not. He's no good to us or this ranch the way he is."

Chris watched them driving nails for a minute or two longer before tossing his hammer back into the tool box and heading toward the house. He had no way of knowing if either of them knew what they were talking about. And there was always the question as to whether or not falling in love with a Yankee would keep him out of heaven. But he was aiming to find out.

******

Bruiser had been cooped up inside the corral for most of the three weeks Chris had spent convalescing, and made short order of the eight miles into Hills Ferry. The man who'd taken over Reb's livery stared at him like he'd seen a ghost, and didn't say much as Chris left Bruiser in his care. He took Johnny's advice and had his Sunday go-to-meeting clothes tucked inside his saddlebags, so the first place he headed was the barber's to get cleaned up. Several folks along the way stopped to stare, and some even stepped off the sidewalk. He was starting to get right peeved by the time he reached the barber shop, and that barber himself began acting strangely, when he saw Chris enter his shop. But, like most barbers, he prided himself on his conversation. He was about the put the razor to Chris' face when he opened up about what was bothering folks.

"It's just a shame, isn't it?"

"What is?" Chris said, opening one eye to watch the razor in his hand.

"About what happened to that pretty woman friend of yours, Mrs. Shafer."

"What happened to Mrs. Shafer?" Chris snagged onto his wrist as the razor moved toward his face.

"Why, she got attacked down by the river this morning, and robbed of all her money. Didn't you know?"

"No I didn't know," Chris said, bolting from the chair. "I just got into town. How could I know?" He gave his face a quick swipe with a towel to remove the lather and strapped on his gunbelt.

"Where is she now?"

"Over at the parson's house," he said, pointing with a shaking finger. "From what I understand, she's been claiming it was those two men who have been giving you the trouble -- Frank Sorenson and Bill Grant."

"Figures." He shoved his hat down tight and paused at the door. "Got any idee how she might be?"

"Not really. I didn't see her personally, and you know how people talk. Some are saying one thing, and others are telling a completely different story. I hear she's a might beat up, and her dress got torn, but," he added as Chris opened the door, "from what I hear, she put up a pretty good fight. Someone said Frank looked as though he'd been caught in a barbed-wire fence."

"Good for her," he said with a nod. "You hang onto my grip. I'll be coming back for that shave and a bath later on."

******

"I guess you heard, didn't you?" Reverend Gibson said as he opened the door.

"Just now, over at the barber's. I'd come for a different reason. Where is she?"

"In the parlor. Better brace yourself," he said with a crooked grin. "The doctor said there's no real damage, but she took quite a beating trying to hang onto that handbag of hers."

Mary Shafer looked up as Chris entered the room, then quickly turned away. But that little glance was enough to let Chris know the parson was right. He also reckoned he had seen a whole lot worse, having spent close to six years with Yankee lead as thick as gnats around a mound of corn mash. But the right side of Mrs. Shafer's face was puffed-up black and blue, and her left eye was almost swollen shut. He couldn't remember having said it, but William told him later that Chris had done some swearing when he saw her sitting near the window. He did remember kneeling and taking hold of her hand.

"The feller at the barbershop said it was Frank Sorenson and Bill Grant that done this to you. Is that true?"

She only nodded and kept her face turned away.

"How'd it happen? What were you doing at the river all by yourself?" Chris almost shouted.

"Not now, Mr. Baker," Velma Gibson said, placing a hand on his shoulder. "She won't be able to answer your questions. The doctor gave her some laudanum to calm her down."

"That still don't answer my question. Why'd y'all let her go wandering off like that by herself?"

"They had no idea I was gone," Mrs. Shafer said in a calm voice. The parson's wife raised her eyebrows and shrugged as Mrs. Shafer continued.

"Velma was at the post office, and Reverend Gibson was visiting a sick parishioner at the edge of town. The bank draft had cleared, and I had gone to see about buying tickets for our return to New York."

"Were you with her, boy?"

"No, sir. I was here watching Edith. I didn't know anything about it, until someone brought her to the front door. They said they'd found her wandering down the street

Poverty Flat

with her clothes half torn off." Chris noticed the boy had the Remington leaning within arms-reach against the wall next to where he was standing. There wasn't a doubt in his mind it was loaded.

"They did that to you, Mrs. Shafer? Tore your clothes off?"

She refused to answer at first, and kept her face turned toward the window. Chris took her by the chin and forced her to look at him.

"Did they tear your clothes off of you?"

"Yes, but its not as bad as it might sound."

"Then tell me what happened," he snapped.

"They…they saw me walking toward the dock, and one of them grabbed me and drug me into the bushes. I…I…tried screaming, but he had his hand over my mouth. The one named Frank kept tearing at my clothing while the other one took the money from my bag. Then…Frank forced me to the ground and…and tried…" she left off with a sob and covered her face with her hands. "I scratched his face something fierce and ran away."

"Good for you," he said, kissing her bruised cheek. "Sorry, Ma'am," he added as she jerked around with a shocked expression.

"Where are them skunks at now?" Chris asked.

"Down at the saloon," William said. "I can see the door from here, and they haven't left yet."

Chris leaned around to look, and as the boy said, he could see the front door to *The Nugget* from the Gibson's parlor window.

"How come they ain't in jail?"

"The sheriff and constable are both out of town, and no one knows when they might be back," Reverend Gibson said.

"Well, it's been a long time since I've seen the inside of a saloon. I reckon I just might wander over to *The Nugget* and have me a little confab with them snakes."

"No!" Mrs. Shafer grab hold of his wrist. "I'm sure they only did this to get you angry enough to go after them."

"Well, I'll tell you what, Ma'am, it shore worked, because I am plenty mad right this minute. And I'm shore going after them."

"No, please don't, Mr. Baker." She tried hanging onto Chris' arm as he moved toward the door.

"Ma'am?" Chris said, prying her hand away. "Now, you know there ain't no one inside this here house that's gonna be able to stop me from going after them devils, don't you?"

"Please listen to me," she cried. "They only want you to go after them so they can kill you. Can't you see that?"

"Yes, Ma'am. I can see that. Only thing is, we Bakers take a sight of killing. They should've known that when I didn't die after they shot me in the back. So, unless the Good Lord says it's my time to go, I don't figure I'll be doing any dying today."

"But, you might kill them…"

"Yes, Ma'am. Unless they're willing to go lock themselves in jail, which ain't likely, I probably will kill them. But it won't be for hate, or nothing they might've done to me. It will be for you and every other decent woman in this town."

"And that's supposed to make it right?" She yelled in his face.

"No, Ma'am, I ain't saying it's right. All I'm saying is, that's the way it is. For some reason, them fellers got filled with poison, and there's just no talking to them. This here gun is the only thing they'll be listening to."

"If you go out that door," she pointed, "and you kill either one of those men because of what they did to me, then I don't ever want to see you again."

"Well, now. That puts another twist onto things, doesn't it? But, my ma always said the Baker men were mule-headed, and I figure I've got to do what is the decent and logical thing to do."

Poverty Flat

"I mean it, Christian Baker. Don't you dare go to that saloon looking for those men!"

Chris laid his palm against her bruised cheek and smiled. "I reckon it's goodbye then. Because I've only been putting off what them fellers started back when we first stopped off for grub in Dutch Corners. I've tried turning the other cheek, ignoring them, and even slapping some sense into them, and nothing seems to work. It's only going to get worse, and next time some one like you, or the boy, could get really hurt. I don't take no great pleasure in killing...never did. And I was hoping you, of all people, would have known me well enough to understand why I've got to face them."

"I mean it! If you kill them I don't ever want to see your face again," she screamed, as he closed the door.

Chapter 24

Chris was about halfway to the *The Nugget* before he calmed down enough to start thinking clearly. He paused at the edge of the main road to check the loads in his Colt, and put a round into the sixth chamber, which he always kept empty for safety reasons. Then, re-holstering the pistol, he turned and headed the opposite way toward the livery.

It wasn't that he was afraid of facing those two inside the saloon, he reasoned. And, having spent most of six years fighting Yankees, he certainly wasn't afraid of dying. But it didn't make any sense getting himself killed over a hot-tempered Yankee female, especially since she didn't want him defending her honor. So, Chris decided he wasn't going to bother defending her honor or anything else about her. Frank Sorenson and Bill Grant could have her, and good riddance. As ornery as she was, they deserved each other. Frank and Bill would probably be begging Chris to take her back after a couple of days of listening to her argue, but the way he felt, there wasn't any way he was going to get back involved with that hellcat. She hadn't caused him anything but trouble from the first day he'd laid eyes on her. That shotgun in her hands should've told him as much.

He had almost gotten to the livery when he remembered leaving his grip at the barber shop. So Chris turned and headed back to the barber's, thinking he had completely lost his mind, and that it was that woman's fault. Then, figuring there wasn't any use in wasting a long trip into town, he plopped back into the chair and got a haircut, shave, and a hot bath in the back room. With a clean shirt and britches, Chris thought he made for a right pleasant-looking fellow if he did say so himself.

Deciding to make the best of it, he headed toward the Chinaman's and had a dinner of funny-looking noodles, rice and pork cooked up in a sweet, red, sticky gravy. It didn't resemble anything his ma ever put on the table, or anything he had ever eaten in the army, but he thought it was right tasty just the same. Chris washed the meal down with hot tea, and the Chinaman gave him a cookie with a little note tucked inside, saying he was about to find true love in his life. He decided that whoever had written that note didn't have a clue as to what they were talking about, or perhaps he was about to find himself a good hound dog like the one he had back home before the war against the Yankee aggressors.

Chris paid the Chinaman for the meal and headed toward the livery. He was saddling Bruiser when Reb and Johnny Garcia came riding in.

"Well, whadda you think, Johnny? Is he already hitched to that woman, or did she run him off?" Reb said as he leaned forward in the saddle.

"I'd say he got cold feet and never told her how he felt, or asked her to marry him," Johnny said.

"Yeah, yer probably right," Reb said as he slid out of the saddle.

"What are you two doing here in town? I thought you were supposed to be building a corral," Chris growled.

"We're finished with the corral," Johnny said as he unsaddled his pony. "And it didn't take us long, once we got you out of our way."

"You saying I don't know nothing about building corrals?"

"No," he shook his head, "but you're not much help when you're moping around like a lovesick puppy."

"Well, whether he's gotten himself a bad case of cold feet or not, this trip into town ain't been a total loss," Reb said, eying Chris up and down. "He's gotten himself all cleaned up. Maybe he'll find a woman on the way back home, or that little sister of your'n might take a shine to him."

" Cola`we's young, but I think she's smarter than that." Johnny laughed.

"Go ahead and have your fun. But there ain't gonna be no wedding between me and that crazy Yankee now or ever," Chris said, and gave the cinches a tug.

"You two had another row, did you?" Reb fished inside his pocket for his plug of chew. "What about this time?"

"She went and got herself robbed and roughed up by Frank Sorenson and his friend. Then, when I was fixing to go give them a lesson in manners, she got all het-up and started yelling at me. Then, she got down right nasty and said things like iffin' I was gonna shoot either one of them skunks, she weren't gonna talk to me no more. So, I just decided she could go sweet-talk them fellers all she wants by her lonesome, and see how far she gets, 'cause I ain't gonna go getting myself shot for no woman that don't want my help."

"Well, I reckon that does shed another light on things, don't it," Reb said thoughtfully, and spit. "But yer gonna have to shoot them fellers one way or another, whether she's involved or not, 'cause there's too much bad blood between you, and they's just dying to see which one is the fastest."

"I reckon yer right, Reb. But if I went bracing them fellers right now, she'd think I was doing it for her. Then, she'd get all het-up again."

"Well, wouldn't you?" Johnny said.

"Wouldn't I what?" Chris said, shoving his hat to the back of his head.

"Be facing those two for her."

"Not likely. And I ain't a gonna be facing them today, just so she won't be thinking I am."

Poverty Flat

"But you will be doing it because of her, no matter when you face them. Don't you see?" Johnny said with grin and a snicker.

"No, I don't see, you smart-alec Injun. What are you talking about?"

"From the first time you had trouble with those two, it was because of the woman. You said so yourself. And every time since, she has been involved in some way. Am I right?"

"Not when they shot me in the back."

"I'm not so sure. She was out at your place, wasn't she?"

Chris nodded.

"I'll bet you this pony against your horse that Frank's being jealous of her was at the root of them shooting you. And, what's worse, you're stuck on her, Mr. Baker, whether you know it or not," Johnny said.

"Alright, have yer laugh." He led Bruiser toward the door and climbed into the saddle. "But try this one on for size. I ain't a gonna be bracing them a'tall, 'cause I'm leaving this here burg. And you can tell them scum-sucking pigs if they want any part of me, they'd better be coming out to the ranch. And if they do, they'd better be prepared to get themselves a bellyful of lead."

"And," he added as he turned Bruiser, "you wanna see how stuck I am? You can tell that female Yankee I said goodbye and good riddance."

******

He had ridden as far as Dutch Corner before catching control of his temper. He stopped Bruiser at the watering trough and sat mulling things over. Reb was right about one thing. Chris *was* going to have to brace them one way or the other. And it didn't make any difference what Mary Shafer or her children thought about it. Frank Sorenson was all swollen up and full of poison. And while Chris reckoned

Billy Grant might not be as poisoned as his friend, he would follow along with anything Frank might say or do, even if that meant getting himself killed. So, deciding today was as good a day as any to get it over with, Chris turned Bruiser back toward Hills Ferry.

It was nigh onto sundown when Chris reached the edge of town. Instead of riding right down the middle of the street like he'd planned on doing, Chris turned out into the wooded area that lay behind the parson's place, and circled the town toward the river. Dismounting, he led Bruiser through the trees with the intention of tying him in the woods, and entering *The Nugget* from the rear of the building. He was almost parallel with the parson's when he heard the shouting. Drawing his forty-four, he allowed Bruiser to trail in behind as he turned that way.

Chris reckoned they couldn't see him as long as he kept in the shadows, but he had a clear view of the parson's from where he knelt in the oaks. There they were, as bold as brass, standing by the front porch arguing with Mrs. Shafer. Chris had to hand it to the little woman. Not only was she telling them he wasn't there, but she let them know under no uncertain terms she wanted all her money back then and there. Frank and Bill weren't having any part of what she was saying, and the thing that set Chris' blood to boil was that they had Johnny Garcia with them. From the look of him, he had taken another beating.

"You tell Nails if he wants to see this boy alive, he'd better get out here now," Frank said, as he shoved his gun to Johnny's head.

"Please, why won't you listen? Mr. Baker isn't here! He left hours ago," Mrs. Shafer yelled. Chris could see Mrs. Gibson tugging on William in an effort to get the boy inside.

"She's telling ya the truth." Reb came into the light from the opposite direction, and from the look of him, Chris decided he had gotten himself a bath and shave also. Reb already had his gun drawn and hanging at his side.

Poverty Flat

"The captain had himself a row with this here Yankee and lit out for his ranch. He said to tell you if you want a piece of him to head out that way, and he'll be right accommodating."

"That so?" Bill said.

"Yeah, that's so. Now let the boy go," Reb said, and pointed his gun.

Chris had seen more than his share of gunplay in his day, but Frank was surprisingly fast as he turned and fired. His shot knocked Reb to the ground before he had a chance to pull the trigger. A split second later, the parson came through the door with a shotgun, but he was met by a bullet from Bill's forty-four. He staggered backward to fall inside the door. Mrs. Shafer yelled like an angry bobcat, and leaped from the porch in an effort to scratch Frank's eyes out.

"Hey!" Chris yelled and drew his gun. Bill jerked around and sent a bullet that buzzed past Chris' ear. He returned the favor with a shot that pitched him backward to land near where Reb was struggling to his feet.

Frank gave Johnny a shove that caused the boy to fall in the dust Chris' in direction, and promptly whacked Mrs. Shafer across the cheek with his pistol. She covered her face with a whimper, and he grabbed her around the waist with his left arm, firing as he drug her inside the house.

Chris ground his teeth as he stared at the door. Now, he was faced with what he had been afraid of happening with Richard Collings that day at Poverty Flat, only more so. Instead of her and the kids being holed up inside a house with a knife-wielding killer, Frank also had the preacher and his wife. Although Chris had no idea what condition the preacher might be in, it still wasn't the best situation he had been hoping to face.

Chapter 25

He ran to crouch beside the open door as the yard filled with people from town, trying to see what the ruckus was about.

"Ain't much of a way to treat a lady, Frank. Wanna let them folks go, and try doing something like that to me?" he yelled. Johnny scrambled on all fours out of the line of fire, over to where Reb was going through Billy's pockets.

"Na, pistol-whipping you ain't what I've been wanting to do, Nails. Seems you kinda got me in a fix, though. I'm stuck here inside this house, and I know you're gonna plug me when I come through that door. Except I might just decide to blow this here woman's brains out first. Then, I got me a couple of snot-nosed kids and the preacher's wife. I just might decide to do for them, also. That is, unless you're willing to talk turkey."

"How's the preacher doing?"

"He's breathing. But he won't be for long, if you don't stop jawing."

"Okay, I'm listening."

"Toss your gun inside, and step back away from the door."

"Then what?"

"Then, I'll come out by my lonesome, and it'll be just you and me, like it was supposed to be from the beginning."

"Well, now," Chris said with a laugh. "That don't sound quite fair. Here I'll be, with nothing but my bare hands, and you'll be bracing me with your iron."

"It's either that, or I'll start tossing these folks out dead, one by one."

"I think you mean that."

"You bet I do, Nails. Now, what's it gonna be?"

"No, Chris! Don't listen to him!" Mrs. Shafer yelled, followed by another slap.

"Shut up, you stupid bitch! Now, get over there by the preacher and say your prayers." Chris could see her through the open door as he gave her a shove. She might've had tears running down her face, but she wasn't crying out loud as she knelt beside Velma Gibson and glared back at him.

"Time's wasting, Nails. What's it gonna be?"

"Okay," he said, and tossed his gun through the door. He hadn't a clue what he was going to fight him with, but as Chris saw it, he didn't have any choice.

"Good boy. I didn't think you had it in you, Nails. I was already figuring on having to kill me a bunch of folks. Now, I want Reb's gun also."

"What for? Reb ain't got nothing to do with this. It's between you and me."

"Hardly. Reb's your friend, and there ain't nothing keeping you from using his iron. Besides, since I can't see him, I don't know if he's still breathing, and I ain't a-trusting him none, especially after him coming and bracing us with that hogleg of his. If he's still alive, tell him to toss it in here, or you do it now! Or I'm gonna blast the preacher's wife right quick."

"I hear ya, Frank," Reb yelled. Then he came closer and gave his pistol a toss, where it rattled and banged across Velma's wood floor. "You crazy sidewinder."

"Here," Johnny whispered, as he shoved Billy's forty-four into Chris' hand. Then, he scampered back to crouch near the porch, where he picked a good-sized rock from the ground.

"Ya know, I'll admit I'm a little slow remembering some things, Frank, especially things a feller wants to forget," Chris said in a loud voice.

"That so?"

"Yeah, and it took me a while to remember where and when I'd first seen you. But when I saw you pistol-whip Mrs. Shafer, it all come back to me. I remembered seeing you down in Fredricksburg at the start of the war. You almost got yourself hung for taking a pistol to the face of a woman you claimed had cheated you out of some money."

"That stinking rotten whore did cheat me, and deserved everything she got," he yelled from inside the house.

"Well, the way I figure it, the only two things that saved you from getting stretched was the war, and the fact that the woman was a tainted lady working in the gambling hall. Fact was, Frank, you considered yourself to be some great shakes with a gun back then, and was claiming to have killed four or five men before the war even started."

"I've added to that number since then, Nails. And I'm planning to add your name to the list before I go. Got any last requests?"

"Maybe, but I didn't trust you then, and I ain't bound to now."

"Aw, that's too bad," Frank said with a laugh. "Ya know, Nails, this kind of talk is starting to bore me. How about you backing away from the door while I come out? Then we can continue talking over old times."

"Okay, you got what you wanted," Chris said, and backed off the porch. He was holding Bill's gun against the back of his leg out of sight, with the hammer cocked.

"Alright, Nails. Here I come."

Chris watched through the open door as he grabbed Mrs. Shafer by the hair and jerked her toward the door in front of him. He cringed as Frank pointed the gun past her shoulder, not leaving him any target at all, except for the woman. Chris figured he was a gonner for sure, until he heard the crack of the Remington.

Frank groaned and let go of Mrs. Shafer's hair as he staggered forward. She crumbled into a ball and rolled out of the way to huddle against the wall. Frank whirled to point his gun back inside the house about the same time Johnny bounced the rock off his ear. He let out a howl and fell against the doorjamb, cussing like a madman.

Chris was surprised the man was still on his feet, and guessed that was why he was planted in the yard like a signpost, when Frank whipped the gun around and fired. The saving difference was that Chris was turned sideways, while Frank faced him square on. Frank's shot tore through Chris' shirt, and burned across his chest, while Chris' first bullet hit Frank's left shirt pocket and slammed him against the doorpost. He staggered forward and tried raising his gun in an effort to get another shot off. Chris fired twice more, with each bullet landing no more than an inch from the first. Frank fell, where Reb grabbed the gun from his hand. Then, when Frank moaned and tried to move, the old warrior placed another round into his head for good measure.

Chris glanced at the crowd gathered in the parson's yard, figuring Dick Purvis and Tom Cunningham would have all the witnesses they wanted. He had a bitter taste in his mouth as he retrieved and holstered his own gun. William was standing where the parson lay, still holding onto the Remington.

"Ya done good, boy," Chris said, slapping him on the shoulder. "Your shooting probably saved yer ma's life."

Chris had done about everything he knew to avoid gunplay, but figured some folks like Frank and Bill seem inclined to fork the devil's bronc and ride it all the way to hell. Mrs. Shafer bolted from where she was on the steps and threw herself at him. Chris started to run, thinking she might be angry, and intending to scratch his eyes out. But she instead threw her arm around his waist and buried her face against his chest crying.

"Ya alright?" he asked Reb, as he stroked the back of her head.

"Yeah. Just got me a new belly button, way off to one side," he said, removing his hand to reveal a bloody patch on his left side. "It'll take more than this little hole to stop me. How's the preacher?"

"Reckon you'd better find out," Chris said. He figured he was gonna be tied up awhile the way Mary Shafer was still clutching him. It was Johnny who found the doctor and helped usher him through the crowd and into the house. Chris knew it couldn't last. But feeling her warm body pressed against his felt mighty good for the time being.

Chapter 26

"Hope you don't mind me saying you surprised me some, Ma'am," Chris said, and took a sip of coffee. They were perched on the steps while the doctor was busy patching Reverend Gibson inside the house. The doc said he didn't think Reb's wound was life-threatening and said he'd have to wait until he'd finished tending to Reverend Gibson. It was Mrs. Shafer herself who wrapped a bandage around his ribs to stop the bleeding, until the doctor had time to look at his wound. The crowd in the front yard had long since hauled Bill and Frank to the undertaker and gone back to their drinking, and whatever they were doing before things got nasty.

"What makes you say that, Mr. Baker."

"I didn't think you'd be talking to me, the way you was pitching a fit when you thought I was gonna go brace them two inside the saloon."

"I was afraid you might get yourself killed." She stared at him for awhile before continuing.

"You still don't understand, do you?"

"Only that there wasn't no way them two would've killed me in a fair fight."

She sighed deeply and stared toward the river. "They almost did, Mr. Baker. That tear in your shirt, and that ugly mark on your chest tells me that much."

That gave Chris something to chew on. So, they sat in silence for a long minute before Chris got the courage to ask the question he didn't really want answered.

"Reckon you'll be going back home to your mama and daddy now?"

"No, I don't believe I will be leaving, Mr. Baker."

"Huh?" He snapped around to stare.

"I said, I don't believe I will be returning to New York to live with my parents."

"I heard what you said, but it don't make no sense," Chris said. Reb and Johnny both glanced at each other and back at the two as they started laughing.

"What doesn't make any sense, Mr. Baker?"

"You're not going. I thought that was what you wanted. You even wrote your daddy asking for money, and he sent it."

"I realize that. But I can always send the money back with a letter of explanation, which is what I plan on doing, first thing in the morning."

"Well, why ain't you going?" Chris tossed the remnants of his coffee in the yard and set the cup on the porch.

"Because I've changed my mind." She grinned at him for a long minute before continuing.

"I'm a landowner, Mr. Baker. I have Poverty Flat to consider. It still belongs to me."

"Well, if that's what's holding you back, I'll buy it from you. You offered to sell it to me, remember? Besides, I'm running cattle on it right this minute."

"I realize that. Which reminds me, you owe me money."

"I what?"

"Owe me money for grazing my grassland. I think the going rate is something like twenty five cents an acre, which comes to two-hundred and fifty dollars, if I'm not mistaken," she said with a nod.

"I'll get your money first thing when the bank opens. But my grazing your land ain't no reason for you to be staying here. You should know I wasn't gonna cheat you none."

"No, Mr. Baker, I never believed you would have cheated me out of two-hundred and fifty dollars. In fact, I'm sure I owe you much more than that for your generosity toward me and my children. I just think it's time I settled down and made a home for my children. William is a growing boy, and he needs a place to call home. I see no reason why Poverty Flat cannot become home."

"Because there ain't nothing there," Chris snapped.

"There certainly is something there, Mr. Baker. It is valuable grassland, and you've got cattle there now. And, if I'm not mistaken, so do I."

"I beg your pardon?"

"You have my cow grazing among your cattle, don't you?"

"Yes, Ma'am, I reckon I do," he said with a laugh. "But I wouldn't call one milk cow a herd."

"No, but you have to start someplace, don't you? And I hope to purchase other cattle with my money. I might even take cattle in lieu of money for grazing rights. That way I'll be building a herd of my own."

"And what are you going to do for a living in the meantime?" He thought the woman was sounding crazier by the minute.

"I'm a fine seamstress. I might open a little shop right here in Hills Ferry. I'm not totally helpless, Mr. Baker, regardless of what you might think. There are a lot of things I can do."

"Okay, I reckon you've answered some of my questions," Chris said, shifting to stare her in the face. Her right cheek was discolored and swollen from getting whacked a second time by Frank's gun, but he couldn't help thinking she was downright beautiful, sitting in the moonlight. "You've got that hunk of land, and you're gonna build a herd, and make a living sewing clothes. But you still haven't said what changed your mind to start thinking like this."

"You did, Mr. Baker."

"Me?" His voice came out high and squeaky, causing Johnny to burst out laughing.

"Yes, you. You helped me decide to stay in California, instead of returning to New York." She stood and brushed the wrinkles from her skirt.

"You see, Mr. Baker, I haven't felt safe since leaving my parent's home. That is, until meeting you. I know this is going to sound bold, but I have decided this is a bold country, and one must be bold to settle here. You happen to be the kindest, most generous, and honest man I have ever met, outside of my father. And William needs some one to look up to. So does Edith." She paused to smile.

"In short, they need a father, Mr. Baker, and I need a husband. I have decided you are the one to meet those needs. Now, if you'll excuse me, I need to check on the children and see how Reverend Gibson is doing."

He sat frozen to the porch, watching the door she'd disappeared behind as Reb grabbed his side, laughing.

"Ow! Danged, but that hurts," he said taking a deep breath. "Looks like we're fixin' to have us a wedding, Johnny. And the way those two get along, that ranch is gonna be one fun place to live on when they get together. Oooo-weee! It'll be the North against the South all over again."

THE END

Author's Notes

Poverty Flat

Poverty Flat Road undercrossing is located approximately three miles south of the Newman exit on Interstate 5 in Northern California. The land consists of approximately a thousand acres of grassland, with no natural supply of water. Ownership of Poverty Flat has changed hands several times, with the land being used mainly for grazing cattle.

Hills Ferry

Judge D. D. Dickerson of Stockton built a ferry crossing on the San Joaquin River in 1850 to encourage trading with Merced County. Jesse Hill purchased the ferry in 1852 and built a hotel, a store and a warehouse. He conducted the ferry for ten years before selling it to William and Richard Wilson. A large Hills Ferry Hotel was added in 1862.

From its beginning, Hills Ferry became a popular river crossing for Mexican immigrants coming into the valley through the Pacheco Pass, and a hangout for tough characters, including Joaquin Murrietta, who made it his headquarters from time to time.

Hills Ferry was considered by many to be the best up-river shipping point, and attracted Simon Newman, who purchased a store in 1870 with the Kahn brothers. The men soon ventured into wheat, sheep and cattle, and even purchased an interest in the steamboat *Continental*, which ran between Hills Ferry and Stockton.

The population doubled by 1877 to over 500, and the town had two hotels, two blacksmith shops, three livery stables, several stores, four saloons, and a number of smaller businesses. It also had more than its share of murders, robberies and assorted crimes. People reported seeing bodies cast from the upper floor of a hotel into the San Joaquin River on several occasions.

For all its history, Hills Ferry no longer exists. Hydraulic and placer mining in the hills soon polluted the rivers with mud and silt, causing steamboat traffic to become dangerous, if not impossible. The establishment of the railroad in 1888 drove the final nail into the coffin, and Hills Ferry was torn apart, board by board, and moved to the present day location of Newman, name for its founder, Simon Newman.

Dutch Corners

Like Hills Ferry, Dutch Corners exists only in memory. A German butcher named Ernest Voight purchased 16 ¾ acres two miles east of Hills Ferry from William Wilson for $340. He opened a butcher shop, a saloon and a road house, calling the small community *Dutch Corners*, then built a race track. While the butcher shop and saloon ran a brisk business, servicing the neighboring ranches and community, it is believed Mr. Voight made a small fortune from his race track.

Sheriff Tom Cunningham

Sheriff Cunningham of San Joaquin County chased Richard (Dick) Collings across county lines for the August 18, 1875 killing of John Sheldon, a sheepherder. The two were friends, but had been drinking, when Collings became angry and killed Sheldon with a knife. Sheriff Cunningham caught Collings hiding inside a coal mine on Mt. Diablo, and hung him.

Captain Rufus Ingram's Rangers

During the Civil War, California's population was an estimated 400,000, of which 40,000 were rebel sympathizers. The rebels were called *Secesh* men, or *Copperheads*. Although they were greatly outnumbered, they preached their southern beliefs openly. Without question, the most daring act by California's *Secessionist* movement was the organization of a band of Confederate guerrillas by Captain Rufus Ingram, Confederate States of America. He, along with Thomas Poole, a former under-sheriff of Monterey County, began recruiting sympathizers in the Santa Clara Valley in 1864.

Their objective was a bold one. They planned to conquer Mexico, establish slavery, then annex it into the Union as a new slave state. The plan was so bazaar that few took them seriously, but by the outbreak of the Civil War in 1861, the *Knights of the Golden Circle* had 16,000 members, who met secretly in small groups to escape detection, using an elaborate system of secret signs and passwords. While some went about raising money, others were plotting to overthrow the state government in Sacramento.

The ninety ton-schooner named the *J. M. Chapman* left the dock at San Francisco on March 14, 1863, and sailed toward the open seas. The ship was heavily armed with cannons, and once the ship was clear of the harbor, they planned to throw the cargo overboard and hijack the first three eastbound mail steamers laden with gold and silver. They would then circle the Horn and deliver their booty to the Confederacy. But their navigator, William Law, lost his nerve and turned them in. They were stopped and arrested before reaching open sea.

While actively promoting his Confederate ideals, Ingram waited to join the *Golden Circle* until early 1864.

Being a former member of William Quantrill's guerrilla band, he quickly became a leader, in command of a guerrilla band of his own. On June 21, 1864, they held up two Concord coaches carrying bullion from Virginia City to Placerville and Lake Tahoe. The combined take was an estimated $26,000 in bullion, with an added $700.00 in coin. Ingram, wanting to make a show, left the drivers a signed receipt bearing his name.

Ingram made little show of hiding his activities, and thumbed his nose at the law, until meeting Sheriff Hall of San Jose on August 5, 1864. Ingram's band had been staying on a ranch on the Salinas River, fifteen miles south of San Juan Bautista, when Sheriff Hall's posse came upon them. One of Ingram's men, Jim Grant was caught and handcuffed, but was able to grab a shotgun and bolt for the door. He was instantly cut down by Sheriff Hall, while the rest of the gang escaped in a hail of gunfire. Ingram and George Baker fled to Missouri, never to be captured. Tom Poole was later caught and executed at noon in Placerville on September 29, 1865, for the murder of deputy Joseph Staples during a gun battle at the Somerset House, five miles from Diamond Springs. Grant eventually healed from his wounds and was sent to prison in Placerville.

The Indian Question

Since the 1820s, the federal government had adopted a *removal policy* to deal with what they call *the Indian problem*. A permanent "Indian frontier" was created in an area call the *Great American Desert*, where it was believed whites would never want to live. By a long series of treaties, the Indians were moved west of this line to new lands. This had scarcely been completed when, in the 1840s, the expansion to the Pacific made the line obsolete.

California posed a new problem, since it was no longer possible to move the Indians farther west. Many settlers argued that the only solution was to remove them from the face of the earth. Governor Burnett told the legislature that a "war of extermination will continue to be waged between the races until the Indian race becomes extinct," and that it was "beyond the power or wisdom of man" to avert the "inevitable destiny of this race."

The events concerning the California Indians in *Poverty Flat* are well documented, including the murder of Mr. Mann. While California had always been considered *a free state*, and slavery was against the law, native Californians were free game, with a bounty placed on their heads. It was not only legal to kill an Indian, but one could be sold into slavery. Politicians, vying for votes, were willing to pass legislation that not only encouraged this removal process, but in most cases funded it.

The poorly armed Indians were unable to withstand such an assault. Those who were not killed outright or sold as slaves were confined to small reservations where malnutrition and disease took its toll. By 1900, the Indian population had fallen from an estimated 300,000 to less than 15,000, with disease claiming more than 60% of the deaths. Starvation accounted for another 30%, with the final 10% resulting from military campaigns, informal expeditions, and various other forms of homicide. The early reservations became little more than death-camps, and a dark blot on California history.

Major Mitchell is the author of ten historical novels and two children's books. He is a member of The Western Writers of America and lives in Northern California with his wife, Judy. He is a frequent guest speaker at historical meetings and schools on the west coast. He has also written three songs and takes center stage on rare occasions as a singer. More about the author, his books, and contact information and photo gallery, may be found at: www.majormitchell.net.

For more great westerns please visit our website:
www.shalakopress.com

CPSIA information can be obtained
at www.ICGtesting.com
Printed in the USA
BVHW070905150122
626156BV00003B/228